GAUDEAMUS

[LET US REJOICE]

Richard

gaudeamus

Let Us Rejoice

TRANSLATED FROM THE SLOVAK BY

David Short

JANTAR PUBLISHING

LONDON 2018

First published in London, Great Britain, in 2018 by
Jantar Publishing Ltd
www.jantarpublishing.com

Slovak edition first published in 2015 as
Gaudeamus [Radujme sa]

Richard
Gaudeamus [Let us rejoice]
All rights reserved

Original text © Richard
Translation copyright © 2018 David Short
Jacket & book design by Jack Coling

A CIP catalogue record for this book is available from the British Library.
ISBN 978-0-9933773-4-1

Printed and bound in Latvia by JELGAVAS TIPOGRĀFIJA

This story takes place in the late twentieth and early twenty-first centuries, mostly in Slovakia and Czechoslovakia). One will often find here coarse language, explicit sex, bloody and bloodless violence and other crimes.

Inspired by actual events.
What the truth is probably no one now knows.
So this is all a fabrication.

I wish to thank all the members of my family and the many friends who read the book at various stages in its evolution and helped me to understand it better. Several dear people gave me much valuable advice and their unqualified assistance, without which the book could not have come about. I'm happy that they exist.

Dedicated to my dear, kind wife.

[ALCOHOL-BRAIN-CHILDREN-DEATH-DELIGHT-DIGNITY-DNA-ETERNITY-FATHERLAND-FOOD-FORGIVENESS-FREEDOM-FUTURE-GOD-GUILT-HAPPINESS-HATRED-HEROISM-HONOUR-HOPE-*JOY*-JUSTICE-LIFE-LIGHT-LOVE-MEDICINE-MONEY-MURDER-MUSIC-ORDER-PEOPLE-POETRY-POWER-PRETENCE-SEX-SHIT-SUCCESS-TRUTH-UNIVERSE-WAR-WORD]

CONTENTS

INTRODUCTION

This uniquely structured novel takes place in Slovakia, still a relatively new country as an independent entity in Europe, the easterly portion of what was, until December 31, 1992 – only half a lifetime ago – Czechoslovakia. Crudely speaking, people 'know' what and where Czechoslovakia was, but there is still little awareness of what and where Slovakia is – or was, for it was always there, as a geographically, geopolitically or linguistically distinct entity, even inside Czechoslovakia. Time was when it was also, because of Czechoslovakia, part of the Soviet bloc. Hence, for all its distinctiveness, it shared (as we also see within the present book) many of the experiences of any one of the other East-Central European countries – though today these are neither new, nor apparently newly named entities –

within the bloc. In short, for no apparent reason, Slovakia, to the dismay of its people, simply does not register with vast numbers of British people, unlike many much smaller places, from Liechtenstein to Albania. It is not even as if there has ever been a dearth of available information about it, whether coming, in their time, from the pens of such noted historians as Robert Seton-Watson (1879–1951) or such once-popular writers as Elizabeth Kyle (1901–1984) (both Scots; Scots have a natural affinity for other peoples seen, for whatever reason, as under-dogs). The former became 'the friend of the Slovaks', he wrote widely about them[1] and was honoured by them with medals and statues. For her part, Kyle also wrote quite a lot,[2] but did not actually help matters by, however innocently or innocuously, getting many things slightly askew. But such has it always been and still is: the current (as of March 2016) English-language Wikipedia page on Slovakia[3] carries much solid, reliable infor-mation, but also, for example, the bizarre description of the High Tatras (a mountain range called Vysoké Tatry in Slovak) as a town in the north of the country.[4] Other cases have done far greater disservice to the Slovak cause, such as George Carcas's *A Concise Grammar of Slovak* (Pontypridd: Joseph Biddulph, 1997), in which the incorrect and misconstrued information about the language so far outweighs the correct as to render it utterly useless to the relatively small numbers of people who take the trouble to learn the language; there are several good textbooks in existence.

The general situation with regard to knowledge of Slovakia is sure to improve with the growing numbers of modern Slovak literary works appearing in English translation, thanks largely to the efforts of people such as Júlia and Peter Sherwood.[5]

In every respect Slovakia has played second fiddle to Czechia (or the Czech Lands, or the Lands of the Bohemian Crown, or Bohemia and Moravia (and southern Silesia), or, today, the Czech Republic). To take but one odd case: there are in London ten or a dozen streets with a Czech connection, while there have been only two with a (though tenuous) Slovak link – today down to one, Presburg Road, New Malden, and that's technically in Surrey; 'Presburg' is the English mutation of the German name of Bratislava, the Slovak capital, and the context is more Napoleonic than Slovak proper.[6] Here at least it comes out ahead of Liechtenstein or Albania.

Yet for all Slovakia's incomprehensible near-invisibility, it has now become a European industrial powerhouse, producing, for example, more cars per capita than any other country and so many televisions that everyone will have seen one somewhere. Its capital's airport even serves as Vienna's second. All this is down to the political and economic changes that have come about since the break-up of Czechoslovakia, notably the burgeoning of transnational capitalist trade and industry – reflected in the present book by the analogous change of fortune of the protagonist, who becomes an agent-distributor for a particular piece of imported medical high-tech. The broad lines of how his life and career changes and develops with the passage of time and the changing political climate over the years are by no means unique in literature and many of the books from East-Central Europe that have appeared in translation in recent years and cover the same five to seven decades evince some distinct parallels; one thinks of Michal Viewegh's *Bliss was it in Bohemia* (originally *Báječná léta pod psa*) or Antonín Bajaja's *Burying the Season* (*Na krásné modré Dřevnici*) among countless others; both of these are Czech works, the former centred round a glassworks, the latter round the life of an entire provincial town with a digression into – Slovakia, while the present book is rooted in the medical profession, civilian and military.

This book, unlike the other two mentioned, is, for all its brilliantly fantastical outbursts, presented as a quasi-memoir or diary and therefore, being in the first person, it appears to carry a greater authenticity than any story apparently just told about others. Furthermore, a key dimension arises from the – itself not original – premise that it is sex that makes the world go round. Sex in lieu of other forms of human intercourse, sex that is pleasurable, sex that is trivial, sex that is dreamed of, sex that is animalistic and automatic, sex that is an instrument of power and, above all, sex that is violent and dangerous. Being a first-person narrative, it invites the question as to the extent to which it might be autobiographical, but that is strictly immaterial. However, there *is* a thread that is rooted in a specific historical event, well known to the author and one that became particularly notorious, but to identify that at this point would not be appropriate…

Given that, for whatever reason, Slovakia has been such an unknown quantity, the book contains an appendix of items that might mystify, or annoy, the reader by being unknown. There are no indications in the text to show that this or that item has a footnote; the solution adopted is simply to list items in the appendix with a page number to aid their retrieval. That list contains other (Soviet, Czech, …) items that appear in the course of the narrative having had their own resonances in the Slovak context. The list also tends to be maximalist rather than minimalist and so may contain items of which an individual reader might think they were nugatory. The translator merely craves the indulgence of all readers.

DAVID SHORT
Windsor, March 2016

---

1   One thinks, among his key works, of *Racial Problems in Hungary* (1908), *The New Slovakia* (1924) and *A History of the Czechs and Slovaks* (1943). Seton-Watson is of course not the only British historian to have been interested in this particular part of Central Europe.

2   Of her five dozen or more books, several, admittedly largely forgotten (Kyle does not even have a Wikipedia page), have a direct or partial bearing on Slovakia, notably *Mirrors of Versailles* (1939), *The White Lady* (1941), *But We are Exiles* (1942), *The Skaters' Waltz* (1944), *Carp Country* (1946), and *A Stillness in the Air* (1956).

3   https://en.wikipedia.org/wiki/Slovakia.

4   This is in the caption to a photograph of a train that is erroneously described as a 'tram', although the author of the picture describes it comprehensively and correctly as an electric multiple unit (https://www.flickr.com/ photos/philstephenrichards/7173422430).

5   For an account of their activities see http://juliaandpetersherwood.com/.

6   The former Presburg Street in Lower Clapton, E5, has simply become anonymous. For a picture of it see:
    https://www.flickr.com/photos/14583963@N00/5450803797/

LIST OF LATIN EXPRESSIONS
AND PHRASES USED
IN THE TEXT

The Latin tags and quotations appearing in the book (in the order of their occurrence), as scribbled in the 'manuscript', or figuring within the text proper, and remarked on by the doctor's widow.

VANITAS VANITATUM, OMNIA VANITAS (Vanity of vanities, all is vanity)

EO IPSO (By that very fact)

MISERERE (Forgive)

NEMO LIBER EST QUI CORPORI SERVIT (No one is free who is a slave to his body)

MENS SANA IN CORPORE SANO (A healthy mind in a healthy body)

ALMA MATER (Nourishing mother)

HOMO SUM, HUMANI NIHIL A ME ALIENUM PUTO (I am a man: I consider nothing human to be alien to me)

NEMO, NUNQUAM, NIHIL (No one, never, nothing)

MODUS VIVENDI (Way of life)

CARPE DIEM! (Seize the day)

EXEMPLA TRAHUNT (Examples attract)

AQUA VITAE (Water of life)

OBSCURUM PER OBSCURIUS (Explaining the obscure by the even more obscure)

TABULA RASA (A clean slate)

VELOCIUS QUAM ASPARAGI COQUANTUR (Faster than it takes to boil asparagus)

BARBA NON FACIT PHILOSOPHUM (A beard does not a philosopher make)

BEATI PAUPERES SPIRITU (Blessed are the poor in spirit)

OMNIA MEA MECUM PORTO (All my things I carry with me)

AD HOC (For the here and now)

GENIUS LOCI (The spirit of the place)

FABER EST QUISQUE FORTUNAE SUAE (Every man is the architect of his own fortune)

INTER ARMA SILENT MUSAE (In times of war the muses are silent)

IN FLAGRANTE (In blazing [offence])

AD REVIDENDUM (*Au revoir*)

AMICUS CURIAE (A friend of the court)

HOMO HOMINI LUPUS EST (One man is a wolf to another)

IMPERIUM IN IMPERIO (State within a state)

CASTIGAT RIDENDO MORES (Laughing corrects morals)

EST MODUS IN REBUS (There is a proper measure in things)

QUI TACET CONSENTIRE VIDETUR (He who is silent appears to consent)

INTER PEDES PUELLARUM MAGNA VOLUPTAS PUERORUM EST (Between

the legs of girls is the greatest pleasure of boys)

PARTURIENT MONTES, NASCETUR RIDICULUS MUS (The mountains will go into labour, and give birth to a ridiculous mouse)

REQUIESCAT IN PACE (May he/she rest in peace)

PRO PATRIA (For the Fatherland)

MORITURI TE SALUTANT (Those who are about to die salute thee)

BEATAE MEMORIAE (Of blessed memory)

IN VINO VERITAS (In wine there is truth)

UBI PUS, IBI EVACUA (Where there is pus, evacuate it)

DE IURE (By law)

SI TACUISSES, PHILOSOPHUS MANSISSES (If you'd kept silent, you'd have remained a philosopher)

QUOAD VITAM (As far as life is concerned)

PRIMUM NIHIL NOCERE (First, do no harm)

CUM GRANO SALIS (With a pinch of salt)

MEA CULPA (My fault)

AMOR VINCIT OMNIA (Love conquers all)

VOX POPULI, VOX DEI (The voice of the people [is] the voice of God)

PARS PRO TOTO (A part for the whole)

IBIS REDIBIS NUNQUAM PERIBIS (You will go you will never return you will perish *or* You will go, you will return, you will never perish)

ALEA IACTA EST (The die is cast)

GAUDEAMUS IGITUR (Let us rejoice therefore)

AMANTES SUNT AMENTES (Those in love are insane)

MEMENTO MORI (Remember [you have] to die)

REQUIEM (*a hymn for the dead*)

AUT VIAM INVENIAM AUT FACIAM (I'll either find a way or make one)

PER VIAS NATURALES (Through the natural passages)

VENI, VIDI, VICI (I came, I saw, I conquered)

AD LIBITUM (As much as you will)

HISTORIA MAGISTRA VITAE (History [is] the teacher of life)

OMNIA CAUSA FIUNT (Everything happens for a reason)

RADIX OMNIUM MALORUM (The root of all evil)

QUOD ME NUTRIT ME DESTRUIT (What nourishes me [also] destroys me)

NON PLUS ULTRA (The acme)

PANEM ET CIRCENSES (Bread and circuses)

CITIUS, ALTIUS, FORTIUS (Faster, higher, stronger)

MUTANTUR OMNIA, NOS ET MUTAMUR IN ILLIS (All things change and
we change with them)

PARVA LEVES CAPIUNT ANIMAS (Small things amuse small minds)

NAM FUIT ANTE HELENAM CUNNUS TAETERRIMA BELLI CAUSA (Even
before Helen a cunny had been the foulest cause of war)

GENESIS (Creation)

INTER URINAS ET FAECES (Between urine and faeces)

VITA BREVIS, ARS AUTEM LONGA (Life is short, but art endures)

AMORE, MORE, ORE, RE ([A true friend is known] by love, bearing, speech
and deed)

NOS HABEBIT HUMUS, NEMINI PARCETUR (The earth shall have us [...]
No one is spared)

PER ASPERA AD ASTRA (Through hardships to the stars)

PIUM DESIDERIUM (A pious wish)

PERSONA NON GRATA (An unacceptable or unwelcome person)

VICE VERSA (On the contrary)

AUDIATUR ET ALTERA PARS (Let the other party be heard)

IN MEMORIAM (In memory)

PATER INCERTUS ([The mother is always certain,] the father uncertain)

RESPICE, ADSPICE, PROSPICE (Look back, here and ahead)

DE PROFUNDIS (Out of the depths)

PLURALIS MAIESTATIS (The royal 'we')

ALPHA ET OMEGA (Alpha and omega)

ALTER EGO (The other self)

NOSCE TE IPSO (Know thyself)

QUIDQUID LATINE DICTUM SIT ALTUM VIDETUR (Anything said in Latin
    sounds impressive)

TERTIUM NON DATUR (There is no third possibility)

QUO VADIS? (Where are you going?)

AD HOMINEM (To the person)

O TEMPORA! O MORES! (Oh times! Oh morals!)

CONSUMMATUM EST (It is finished)

LOREM IPSUM (a nonsense phrase, untranslatable)

NUNC ET IN HORA MORTIS NOSTRAE (Now even in the hour of our death)

CUI PRODEST (Who gains by it?)

DEUS EX MACHINA (A god out of the machine)

ET TU, BRUTE? (You too, Brutus?)

FIAT LUX (Let there be light)

AD ACTA (To the archives)

PECCAVI (I have sinned)

ORBIS PICTUS (The World in Pictures)

AUT VIVERE, AUT MORI (To live or to die)

CETERUM CENSEO CARTHAGINEM ESSE DELENDAM (Anyway, I think
    Carthage should be wiped out)

DUM SPIRO SPERO (So long as I'm breathing, I can hope)

My husband was a man of dignity.

Of all the qualities particular to people, what always mattered most to him was dignity. But he wasn't that way *because* dignity mattered to him. He was that way because dignity was his way of life. It might be more accurate to say that dignity was his way of despising life, but precisely because he despised life he didn't deem it necessary to advertise his disdain.

In saying that he despised life I don't mean that he wasn't interested in life or didn't love life. But he did pick with care the objects of his interest or love and took great care to conceal his interest. That was the second thing that mattered to him. No one was to be able to tell that this or that mattered to him, that he loved this or that, that he was dependent on this or that.

Because the third thing that mattered to him was independence.

My husband was a doctor. An independent doctor. He had a small surgery in the front part of our house, where he would receive and treat all who showed an interest in his services. He never signed a contract with any insurance company, and he never asked his patients for money. He had no particular specialism and claimed to treat not ailments, but people.

It might seem odd that he should despise people while devoting his entire life to them. But I didn't say he despised people. He despised *life*, existence as such. Most of all he despised its highest form – human society. He treated people because he thought that the most dignified way of passing the time. He often spent the entire day in the surgery, and some nights as well. I believe the main reason he did so was that he was constantly searching for something. In the fates of all the old people, the fathers and mothers, the teenagers and babes-in-arms, the lonesome, the rich, artists, professors and madmen who crossed our threshold he would look for evidence that he was mistaken in his core belief.

He would often tell me about his patients. In the evening, having finished his consultations for the day and eaten a light supper, he would sit with me by the huge fireplace in the living room and paint me pictures of various lives, details of the tiny, major and even monumental battles waged by the human body against the futility of existence and by the human soul against its egocentric essence. He sought in his patients flashes of eternity. For what really interested him was eternity. The eternity that he sought in history, music, art, literature and philosophy.

I know this for a fact, having lived with him for many years. I know it just as I know that he didn't love me. I was his medium, his mamilla, his litter-bin, his vomit bowl, lightning conductor, boxer's bag, his handkerchief for tears and phlegm. I know that he hated me because I was the only form of dependency he was prepared to tolerate.

My husband died today in the small hours.

His body is still lying in our bed, his pale features illuminated by flickering candles. The undertakers will be coming in the morning to take him away. His independence has come to an end, and I have to hand his body over – how comical is this? – to the society that he so despised so that it might dispose of him in a civilised manner, in accordance with the law and public health regulations.

But he's still here. I'm looking at him, at his closed eyes that could see so far, at his mouth that has taught me so much. I'm looking at the bed to which he led me when he was forty-eight and I was barely twenty.

Yes, he hated me. In me he hated everything that he hated about the world and the universe. All the mundanity, baseness, vacuity and filth. He hated me because through that mundanity, baseness, vacuity and filth he saw, as in a mirror, himself; his dependency excoriated him and stripped him of the dignity of which he made so much.

But his loathing was benevolent. No less so than it was absolute, inescapable and devastating. Yet it was also indulgent, condescending and empathic. I was the tunnel joining two universes, I was someone from an alien world and at the same time I was he himself.

I learned that I'd never been my own self. I'd been no beloved treated to flowers and gifts on her wedding anniversary, I'd not been one before whom another kneels and begs forgiveness, nor had I been a beguiling mistress, nor one who had to be fought for; I'd been a fount of neither doubt nor inspiration.

And I've hated him, too. Naturally. For all those reasons. To me our house has been a prison and he my gaoler, a tyrant, a vampire who sucked out of me all that had been young, free and happy. Just as I had absorbed his seed into my body until the day his desire completely died, I also absorbed his resentment, his arrogance, his hollowness. His infinite sadness. Like him, I saw fewer and fewer reasons for *joy*. The only thing I looked forward to was listening to his evening stories about flashes of eternity.

Sometimes he would tell me about the Colleague who would visit him after he opened the surgery. He was actually his first patient. Attempted suicide, post-traumatic stress disorder, secondary asthenic depressive syndrome, toxicogenous complex hallucinations. My husband said that although he wasn't suffering from any physical ailment, he was the most wretched man he had ever known. I believe he was the only living being he ever truly loved.

The undertakers won't be here before morning. This is our last night together. The candles will last till daylight. Just as any other night. In our house there always had to be light, independent, primal, non-electric light. The moment the sun went down, he would light chunky wax candles in the large living room, where there was always a fire in the hearth, then at bedtime we would light two small candles either side of the bed.

Light was the first thing God created, he would say, and God knew full well why. Because the essence of the universe is darkness, the vast majority of the firmament at night is black, and light alone makes any sense of things, light alone is the key, light alone is hope. Yes, "hope" is what he said. If anyone could be said to have lost all hope, as recommended by Dante, it's my husband. Despite that, he would light those candles every night and every night our house would shine out into the universal darkness, as derisive and provocative as the music that came from the Titanic.

There was only one other thing that preceded light in the murk of the universe.

The Word.

He adored literature. Our large house was full of books of every kind. We would read stories, poems, ancient myths. Odysseus, Hercules, Ruslan, Eugene Onegin, Faust, Dorian Grey, Huckleberry Finn... He devoured biographies – from Socrates, Leonidas I of Sparta or St Paul to Tiso, Husák and Válek. And Dubček of course. He would have me read as to a child who wants to hear the same fairy tale over and over again, who would disrupt a puppet show by shouting at Hansel and Gretel not to stray too far as they picked wild strawberries and not to eat of the gingerbread house, and he couldn't wait for Good-for-nothing to become king. He would weep when this or that hero, whether literary or historical, managed to rise up against his fate, against the system, against injustice and he would weep even more when some such hero finally came unstuck because he wasn't strong, tenacious or honourable enough, or when it finally transpired that he was just an ordinary fool, coward or villain.

A word, he would say, is not just a bearer of a meaning, a word represents order, a word finds sense in chaos, a word is Archimedes' firm spot. He experienced sheer delight as he read verse in hexameters or pentameters, he relished the perfect metaphor, he couldn't get enough alliteration, pleonasm, onomatopoeia, anagrams... Time and again he was amazed by the discovery of how a word could, faster than the speed of light, connect seemingly unconnectable worlds, how it could extract the essence of phenomena, how it itself was an extraction that can gratify a soul longing for harmony and mathematical order. This because he didn't see metaphor as an irrational flight from reality, but as the finding of a common denominator, prime number or atom.

Above all he loved puzzles, the tiny hints, pointers concealed in a text: he sought them out as you would seek hidden treasure, falling gleefully into the little traps set by the author, and any time he cracked the secret code, he briefly became another person. At such rare moments he had a sense of fellowship with someone else of this world and I recall a number of pleasant evenings when he opened one of the old wines hidden away in the cellar and treated me to an ecstatic account of his discovery.

"*Šicko so šickim skapčano.*" This 'Everything is connected to everything else' was his favourite saying – always quoted in its alluring East Slovak dialect form, and it filled him with a peculiar sense of satisfaction to find "The Word" in the Bible, Shakespeare, Prévert, Khlebnikov and Válek, to discover that Huckleberry Finn, like Eugene Onegin, lived in St Petersburg, that Finn was also the name of the wise old man who helped Ruslan liberate Kiev from the evil Pechenegs and gave him the magic ring with which he saved Ludmila from the hunchbacked dwarf Chernomor, that the nickname of the Grand Duke of Kiev, Vladimir I, conveyed the brightness of the sun, just like the nickname of Louis XIV, in whose glare France roasted at the threshold of the Revolution of which Chou En Lai, asked about its impact, said that it was too soon to tell, not to mention what one might say of the October Revolution in Russia or November 1989 in Czechoslovakia.

I have taken from my husband's antique wardrobe a thick folder, the book in which his much-loved Colleague set down his life-story. I never met the man and my husband never told me his name, and I never asked. I knew he'd written something and my husband would frequently leaf through the manuscript and make more and more annotations of his own in it. On its cover I saw the title *Gaudeamus*, that's to say 'Let us rejoice'. I'm wondering why the poor man gave his book such an optimistic title. He may have meant it ironically, I muse, given that the old student anthem is really about the transience of life.

My husband never asked me to read this book to him. When he'd finished with it, he always put it carefully away under lock and key. I was jealous, naturally.

Now I have unlocked the wardrobe and taken his secret out.

Gaudeamus igitur.

So be it then – let us rejoice...

I have checked that my husband is properly covered, that the candles are in order, with no wax dripping from them, and that the shutters are closed tight. Now I'm lying next to him on my half of the bed, just like any other time. I have opened the book at the first page and begun to read aloud.

Just like any other time.

GAUDEAMUS

He who tells the truth will not be happy…

NOTEBOOK № 1

Vanitas venitatum
omnium (VANITAS)

Law № 1 says that anything that can expand can also contract. Law № 2 says that any swing will eventually stop swinging.

That fills me with calm and joy. Truth to tell, all my hopes are pinned on these two aphorisms being true.

The first law is calming in itself.

The expanding of the universe will come to a halt. The invisible elastic bands between particles will be stretched to breaking point and then we start going back. Our entire journey following the Big Bang will be repeated in reverse. The universe will go backwards as in a slapstick film. Chickens will re-enter their eggs, and our food will return bit by bit from our mouths onto our plates, where our knives and forks will re-shape them into neat portions. The stars will start moving back towards one another, then they will begin consuming one another until everything shrinks back into a single speck with infinite gravitational pull that will let nothing escape. Emptiness and calm will reign throughout.

And there will be silence. No one will blether on about the future or lie about the past. No one will turn people into Young Pioneers, Young Communists, paid-up members of the Party; partisans, soldiers and generals; Czechs, Hungarians and Russians. No one will be hungry or thirsty. No one will die abandoned, launched into space, incommunicado in exile or prison. No one will get shot or die in a bombing raid. There won't be any dying at all. There'll be no anything at all. All hearts will stop beating, all sperm cells will stop flicking their tails, cell organelles will cease pumping sodium and potassium, calcium will stop caring where it is and the cilia on epithelial cells of all digestive, respiratory and reproductive tubules will finally be able to take a break. Brains will stop churning out ideas and commands. There'll be no new crackpot schemes. The letters in this book will retreat into the keyboard and the paper will be left blank.

No one will kidnap, rape or murder anyone else.

A holy peace will descend.

But the first theorem without a second doesn't go far enough: it is reasonable to fear that anything that has contracted might expand again and so the whole shitty business repeats itself. Which is why Law № 2 is important. Any swing will eventually stop swinging. The frictional motions of the universe will cease. Atoms will stop oscillating, electrons will stop going round and round, electric charges will lose their power. Neutrinos will uniformly fill up space in perfect silent harmony, nothing will move, like dust on the moon or a windless desert…

Everything's fine. It will work out all right. We've nothing to fear…

Let us rejoice!

I was lying on a comfortable double bed and switching between sports channels. For a third time a quiet whirring came from my mobile.

Lucia.

I let it drone on till it stopped. Third time, fourth time and a fifth time. I took a small bottle of sekt from the minibar. The cork gave only a slight hiss in the palm of my hand, I didn't want to grant it that second of fame, that meteoric orgasm, that every cork in a bottle of sect spends all its life waiting for. I poured myself a glass. The cold bubbles tingled in my throat.

I turned the TV off. The white, impersonal walls of the hotel room were not made any the cosier by the modern art or the expensive solid-wood furniture or even the heavy curtains. I was in a cage. I could have got up, gone down to the hotel bar, or the casino, but I couldn't be bothered. After all, it was the same cage.

A text message bleeped. "I suppose you want to be alone. I do understand, but it pains me. I hope you're not intending to harm yourself. I love you. L."

"Sorry," I said back to the still illuminated display, kissed it and clicked *off*.

I knew that Lucia didn't deserve that. I could never repay all that she did for me. Lucia loves me. We're always most callous to those who love us.

Intending to harm myself? Hm, interesting... I'd never given it much thought. That called for some more wine. I rang room service and in no time I had a new, bedewed bottle in a silver bucket of ice. The miniskirted waitress wiggled her hips and smirked. "Will there be anything else?" "Not today, darling."

I hung the 'Do not disturb' sign on the door and, just in case, unplugged the phone.

Right, then. Suicide.

OK, there's no point putting it off. As things are, life is nothing but a desperate attempt to kill time somehow, to find some way to keep our brain cells busy to stop them getting bored. Every part of the body, every organ, works non-stop to keep Mr Brain happy. We read books, go to the cinema, the theatre, engage in sport, travel, cook, drink, smoke, meet up with friends, set up clubs, make love, suffer, write songs, invest, gamble, do research, go on a quest, conduct investigations, write and philosophise, all to give His Majesty something to do.

So what about it? Our allotted span will come to an end, our exhausted cells will stop trying to play catch-up: "All right, you've had your fun thinking stuff up, so now pack your bags, *game over*, *hasta la vista*, *bye-bye*!" A few other brains will kill a moment or two crying and reminiscing, and another few may well be delighted.

Your mark on the universe? Did you invent the aeroplane? Or the mobile phone? Did you send a rocket to Mars, have you ever cured someone of something, have you ever cooked some new dish?

Have you written a good book?

Maybe. It may take the tide some time to demolish your castle and obliterate your footprints in the sand.

But me?

I've invented bugger-all. I was a hospital administrator. We drove a lady Professor out of the clinic, I may have helped the odd patient. And I shagged a couple of chicks.

Three months after I've gone no one will give a damn about me.

Why prolong the agony? Why keep blowing soap bubbles, wondering at how beautiful they are and how high they fly, when they're all going to burst anyway?

I poured myself another glass, held it against the light of the bedside lamp and downed it in one.

And oh dear, yes, I have loved. I did, once way back. With all my heart. All of it. Dear, oh dear...

That took my brain about three-thousandths of a second. It was clear what I had to do, what I wanted to do. Suicide can wait.

I got dressed and grabbed a cab.

To the cemetery.

Miserere

It took me quite a while to find the grave. As if it was hiding from me. *"It must be beyond those trees, I remember..."*

I walked down one path after another, going round in ever increasing arcs, but someone seemed to have put a spell on what had been a familiar spot.

"Are you cross with me, Ľudka? Do you want to punish me? I know I deserve it, but I have to find you!"

It was a warm summer's night, much like back then... Crickets chirped from the endless fields of Southern Slovakia, the sky was ablaze with stars.

Like back then.

"See, you can't even remember where my grave is. What are you really after?"

"Don't drive me away, please don't!"

"Are you here to pay your dues? Assuage your conscience?"

"I'm here because… because I miss you… I'm here because I see your face the whole time. Your eyes that keep surprising me when I'm least expecting it and watch what I'm doing. I know you understand what happened, you understand and accept it. I'm here for you to forgive me…"

Finally I found it. The huge family grave with a photo of Ľudka on the headstone. I had to get quite close and kneel down in order to touch her face and wipe the dust off it with my hand.

I kissed her. The cold stone sprang to life at the touch of my lips.

Or did I just imagine it?

I was like a space ship that had been wandering through the cosmos and had now found its home base. I docked in silence. Now I wanted to remain stock-still. I stood with my gaze fixed on the photo. I felt that familiar tingling, as always in her presence. Nothing vulgar, nothing specific, just a sweet, natural, quiet sensual pleasure. A sense of absolute security and composure. I'm at home here. With you, next to you, in you…

"I'll stay now," I said aloud, "I'm going nowhere."

And at the same time, at that very instant, I realised I was lying.

"Of course you'll go, you obviously won't stay. That's ridiculous!"

I tried to dash aside this importunate call of reality like when the alarm clock rings in the middle of a dream.

"Wake up and have a look at yourself! By tomorrow you'll have sunk back into the sweet swill of your daily life and start supping it like an alcoholic. Stop playing games! Stop talking to spirits!"

"Spirits? No! This is the real me! This, Ľudka, this is me. The rest is just inescapable pretence. My whole life has been a pretence. All my life I've been someone else."

"But that 'someone else' would seem to have been pretty success-ful. You seem to quite like being that other person…"

Tears welled up in my eyes, one spilled over and I felt the tickle of it on my cheek. I didn't wipe it away, it trickled down to my chin and dripped to the ground. It wasn't unpleasant. For the first time in ages I had experienced something real. I wanted to cry properly. I was standing on the cosmic stage, with spotlights on me. Behind the invisible cameras stood the Great Director. How I performed would determine whether he would have me in his play. With a tightness gripping my throat I screamed:

"Save me, my love, save me! Help me break free! Without you I can't. Give me a sign! Let's show them all that I'm not as I seem, let's show them how life should really be lived! We shall be pure and beautiful just as we always were. Prove that you're not just a phantom, that you're not just that for which I'm yearning, that you're no false fata morgana…"

I looked up at the stars, waiting to see if one of them might fall. But the universe just smiled its indifference. It didn't start turning to some different rules. No comet flared, no cross appeared, no *mene tekel*, the tomb remained closed, no light issued from it, and I heard no voices. No one even responded with a "We'll let you know…"

The cold of evening made me shiver.

I have to go back to my shitty life.

I said farewell.

Kissed the photo.

The stone remained cold…

NEMO! liber est qui corpori servit

Today I ought to be celebrating. It was a great day for my business.

I poured another glass, drank a toast to my reflection in the big mirror.

I used to watch Lucia in the mirror, having sex with me. And me having sex with her. It was odd, seeing us from this angle. It was like watching someone else, like being both on stage and in the audience. I could feel Lucia's movements about my groin, at the same time seeing her rearing over the body of some other guy. I studied the curve of her back, her bobbing breasts, I studied our genitals. Usually when making love, one cannot see one's genitals. In the mirror they were quite visible, like in a porn film.

When she first came here, she sat wide-eyed on this king-size bed, naked, playing with my toes. I just loved it. Women know a thousand wondrous things to do with your genitals, they love to play around with your lips and tongue, they stroke their delicate fingers through the hairs on your chest, electrify the thick skin on your back, or dig their nails passionately into it, and they grasp your buttocks with a kind of proprietary entitlement. But few of them know the sheer physical pleasure it can give a man if they apply themselves to his feet. Fondling them, scratching them, splaying the toes, sucking on them, massaging them, nipping them, nibbling them, crushing them together... A few precious exceptions have the knack of isolating every single spot on your foot, between the toes, between the bones and tendons, and opening it up, changing tension and pain into relief and an intense pleasure that you can feel somewhere at the bottom of your brain. The pleasure is only intensified by the rarity of the experience, the fact that the woman you are with is being so attentive to such a remote and despised bit of your body. It is as if she were attending to more than just your body. As if she were uncovering the most secret folds of your inner being, healing the most deep-seated sorrows of your past, breaking down barriers with the accumulated venom, draining gatherings of pus, sweeping away forgotten sediments and treating badly healed scars. It's even better than fellatio. With that you have a sense of superiority, power. But foot massage affords a sense of humility and gratitude. You have placed yourself in the hands of a brilliant higher power, whom you trust more than your lawyer, banker or family doctor. With fellatio you feel guilty. There is that intense pleasure and satisfaction as you hold by the hair the head shimmying away between your legs, but you're not quite sure that it's right. With a foot massage you're completely at ease. There was never anything so unequivocally right, so good, so one-hundred-per-cent okay.

"What have I done to deserve this?" I asked about the only thing that was not clear.

Mens sana in corpore sano

She smiled, drawing back her lush platinum-blond fringe.

"You treated me to a right-royal dinner. You've made right-royal love to me…"

She had a real gift for picking on the right things. Food and sex. The first time I took her down to breakfast in the hotel dining room she helped herself to everything that was available. A slice of every kind of ham and salami, some smoked salmon, an egg stuffed with caviar, potato salad, crab salad, pasta, celery and egg salad, a piece of all eight kinds of cheese, vegetables and pickled onions, grilled aubergine, cereals with strawberry and pineapple yogurt sprinkled with roast almonds and hazelnuts, a croissant with butter and jam, a Danish pastry with vanilla custard and raisins, a piece of Czech poppy-seed tart, apple juice and orange juice, coffee and a glass of oak-aged Australian chardonnay. She even took a bottle of Evian, remarking that she had to try a spring water that cost sixty crowns and was drunk by models, but that was the only item she left, disappointed that it tasted just like ordinary water.

I was smiling. "Don't make fun of me! All this, here… it's awesome… it's paradise!"

I wasn't making fun of her. I was simply pleased, there being no greater pleasure than making a woman happy.

I was recalling my first stay at the hotel, during a training course for The Instrument. I'd done exactly what Lucia had done today, except perhaps for the yogurts and wine. And from my room I'd taken home all the shampoos and soaps and on my way down the corridor I'd even nicked a couple of chocolates from the cleaner's trolley – which subsequently melted inside my jacket pocket.

Unlike me, Lucia wasn't taken ill. When we went for a swim in the hotel pool, I couldn't drag her out of the water and beneath the surface she kept grabbing my prick.

"I don't think I deserve that," I responded. "Certainly not after feeding you and making love to you. People are crazy. They buy The Instrument from me, a ghastly plaything, because it's public money and that gets spent on anything that might prove lucrative. I've got no principles, I pay up. And as for sex, I reckon I get it from you more than giving it to you."

"Ouch!" I yelped with pain, because she had just bitten my big toe. She was laughing.

She sprang up and hurled herself breasts down on my belly.

"Just so's you know," she said slowly, breathless from the leap and twisting a strand of my hair round one finger, "people buy from you because you're a great guy. Because what you sell is good and because you make people happy. With money from you they can also take their wives and girlfriends out for a good dinner and to a good hotel, so you make even more people happy. Stop worrying about something that isn't. Are you a seeker after truth? Just look, this is the truth!"

She stood up so that I could see her perfect body and started dancing slowly to some imaginary music playing somewhere inside her head. Before long I caught the tune as well and joined in. Our movements became synchronised and together we danced the oldest dance known to man. The dance that soothes the hunter's pain and heals his wounds, the dance that re-ignites the fire in a cave and re-fills it with light, *joy* and a feeling that everything may after all make some sense ...

Alma mater

In general terms, it is harder to persuade a woman to have sex than a man. A woman has far more checkpoints to get past on the way to opening up. The female's capacity for reproduction is, in comparison to the male's, conspicuously lower and therefore she has to make a sound choice of partner whose genes allow of being united with hers. Most women manage that once or twice in a lifetime, many never and very few more than five or six times. By contrast men – males – can easily have hundreds of offspring.

A man being considered for sexual partnership is therefore subjected to meticulous and repeated testing, scanning, frisking, evaluation, classification and quantification of everything and anything from how he smells to the size of his bank account. Women keep these processes going from the first encounter on, systematically and unconsciously, irrespective of whether the objective of the interaction being initiated is the begetting of children or not.

The moment all the warning lights go green, the moment the woman's brain approves the man as a suitable father for her children, he ceases to interest her as a man and the only thing she wants then is – intercourse. Sperm. Whatever the initial motive for considering a possible sexual union might have been... And yes, some modern women have their warning lights permanently switched off; but whether the woman is playing the part of wife, mistress, prostitute, or porn-star, at moments of intercourse she will be oblivious to the man.

During those stellar seconds and minutes all women are equally free and pure, totally context-free, the embodiment and condensation of the one important thing in the entire universe, the replication of their DNA. Their whole body mutates into one huge vagina possessed of arms, legs, a mouth and eyes, all of which are in service to what she is doing.

All women, all females in the world slide themselves onto bars that lead to the centre of the Earth and rub themselves against them. By means of this friction, billions of vaginas produce energy each and every day, energy that accumulates deep down and from there, through tiny little conduits, feeds every plant and every animal that lives on the surface. Without this energy nothing grows, nothing lives, nothing can function.

At intercourse a woman is a goddess, mother, queen of the Earth and all creation. A woman's intercourse is sacred. Like the Holy Grail, the philosopher's stone, like the crown jewels or a heart beating in the palm of an open hand. Sacred and inviolable.

He who desecrates female intercourse will arrest the energy flow of the entire Earth.

He who kills another is as having felled a tree.

He who rapes a woman turns a forest into the wasteland in which he himself will perish.

Ah, all this smart talk on the subject of women...

That patient, the Colleague whose book I've been reading, was probably just like my husband. He thought he understood everything, that in the plan of a complex bit of circuitry he could see the mainspring of all human actions.

There was a time when I enjoyed listening to his philosophising.

There was a time...

Now his hand-written Latin tags in the margin of the book... They struck me as infantile. Forced, unbecoming and cold. Ludicrous even. He probably thought them witty or enlightening. I'm sure that's it.

Aphorisms. Latin, Greek, Hebrew. He loved using them and did so frequently, but no, not from some desire to impress, not even me. It was more of a device by which to test and classify people. Anyone who knew them, anyone who understood them apparently understood his secret language, they passed the entrance exam and might seek membership of his elite club.

If truth be told, he was its only member.

He that is without sin among you, let him first cast a stone at me, he would say.

Or: *Nothing that is human is alien to me.*

Yes, he even taught me it in Latin: *Homo sum, humani nihil a me alienum puto.*

He claimed that everyone should understand Latin. Naturally...

He even poked fun at his patients: above the surgery door he fixed Dante's Tuscan *"Lasciate ogni speranza voi ch'entrate"* and waited to see who would get the joke. No one did.

No one, never, nothing.

Nemo, nunquam, nihil...

Only the Colleague.

He understood it and even grasped that it wasn't a joke.

Yes, my husband had an obsession with testing. And anyone else being only rarely to hand, he would test me. The first time I entered his house I had to guess who had painted all the pictures hanging round the living room. I almost bolted there and then. Then came Plato's riddle with the hats, Einstein's brain-teasers, Edison's intelligence test, questions from history, numerical series, geometric figures, or even just the capitals of countries. Burkina Faso – Ouagadougou. Madagascar – Antananarivo. Saint Lucia – Castries.

Maybe I should have left.

Modus vivendi.

Basically, painkillers work according to one of two principles. Either they desensitise the pain-perceiving centre in the brain, or they paralyse the nerve endings at the site of the pain. Nature knows a third way: suppressing one pain by another, greater. A wound has to suppurate till it depurates, an embedded thorn has to become encapsulated, an ulcer scratched raw has to heal to a scar.

Nature needs pain for the body to mobilise its powers of healing and protect itself against further harm. When a pain is no longer useful, the body makes and administers the most effective remedy – endorphins. The pain passes, euphoria takes over. You feel good.

(Except that endorphins, like all opiates, suppress immunity, the ability to differentiate between the good and the harmful …)

I joined a student drama group.

I wanted to do recitations about love; we did plays about Lenin.

I wanted to speak about sorrow; I turned into an optimistic builder of socialism.

I wanted to seek the truth, and found it. The only one.

I was good at recitation. I was nominated to be the culture rep on the faculty committee. The plenary meeting elected me *nem. con.*

From the Universities Section central office I received an invitation to attend a training course.

That's where I met Jano Prcúch.

Jano opened doors to higher offices, allocated funds for university cultural events and Smaragd vouchers for foreign travel. It was good being mates with Jano. Jano saw to it that each training course left a deep mark on the minds of female members of the Socialist Youth Union – SYU. As one of the few male cultural reps I soon realised that, provided I respected his territory, the way to a great future lay wide open before me. As it had for that lady professor in the USSR.

- Comrade Maria Ivanovna, tell us: How can it be that you, a scholar of repute at the Leningrad Institute, became a prostitute?

- Simples – a stroke of luck …

Carpe diem!

The three-day course for the culture reps of faculty SYU committees started with a formal opening session at which Jano had everyone introduce themselves. In the course of this he took detailed notes and spent the next three days in his hotel room, whither he summoned carefully selected female attendees for a private chat.

For dinner we had chicken, specially reared at a nearby cooperative farm and supplied for the occasion at a token cost. The wine, in unmarked bottles, had been drawn that morning straight from casks and delivered in person by the chauffeur of the director of the State Wineries at Pezinok. The chickens were roasted on massive spits set up in the middle of the wine bar. Music was supplied by a folk ensemble, brought in by Jano for that evening only. For some years they had represented Slovak university culture at various festivals. They were just back from Japan.

They really did play well. Together with the wine, the songs from the Upper Hron and Liptov county went to my head. Soon I was singing along with them at the very top of my voice.

Očová zhorela, len krčma ostala, všetci ju hasili…
[Očová burned down, except for the pub, everyone helped put out the fire…]

The chicken was superb. The pickled peppers from Rye Island had been supplied by Jano himself from a festival of Slovak-Hungarian culture. No one pickles peppers like the Magyars.

Mara, moja Mara, sedem bohov tebe, ja som ťa vychoval, a druhý ťa …
[Mary, my Mary, you ungrateful hag, you, 'twas I gave you everything, now you let him …]

"Sod this, let's drink…"

"I say, guys, what was it like in Japan?"

I borrowed an accordion and played along with them. The girls' eyes were full of admiration. We danced, my, we were good!

Ajaju, ajaju, nechytaj ma za ňu…

[Yippee, yippee, yippee, keep your effing hands off me…]

Exempla tralunt

Jano was at a table with a bunch of probably important people. He beckoned me over.

"I say, you're good! How's it going? Do you like the wine?"

"It's pretty good…"

"Spätlese," the winery director's chauffeur said. "Late harvest."

"It's okay, good enough anyway…," I said.

They laughed.

"Making wine's like making love, my friends," Peter Spružina chimed in, a fellow medic from the faculty in Bratislava: "The longer you can put off barrelling it, the sweeter it is…"

"And the longer you can keep it in the barrel, the greater the pleasure when you tap it off," another poet added, a short guy with a huge moustache.

"Though it does depend on the barrel," I found my voice and put in my own sixpennorth.

"You bet," the winery director's chauffeur broke in on the general merriment. "Recently my boss had two hundred second-hand oak barrels brought from Australia… Anyway, Jano, ask about the next tasting…" At which the entire table roared with laughter. "You wouldn't believe the extra flavour you get from a barrel that's been going for twenty years!"

"Listen, do you fancy a job at USCOS?" Jano asked, turning to me while the others were wiping away their tears.

The Universities Section Central Office for Slovakia, the topmost echelon of the Socialist Youth Union where colleges and universities were concerned…

"Doing, like, what exactly?"

"Listen, don't worry, you don't have to do anything, you'll be a member, a member of USCOS. A member for Košice."

"Right, ha-ha… Why not?"

"Good. Let's discuss it tomorrow. Let me introduce you – this is the chairman, Julo Černý."

He was that 'poet'… We shook hands. His years as a student were well behind him, he was teaching at some faculty or other.

"Here's to you!"

Jano filled the glasses of everyone round the table and raised his own: "And to collaboration! Hey, Piťo, play another one, just for the doc here!"

There you have it, I was a member of the faculty committee, previously I'd chaired the class group, but never ever had I been noticed by union HQ in Bratislava and offered the chance to be on the top flight… I didn't know what it amounted to, or what would be expected of me, but whatever it might be I was going to be representing the far east of the country right there in Bratislava!

Then together we launched into "*Na Kráľovej holi…* " – "There's a green tree standing up on Royal Wold," with me pulling the bellows like a good 'un. Let 'em see my calibre and what I have to offer! I had a sense that beneath his whiskers Julo Černý was smiling at me…

Once we'd done with the folksongs, the disco could start.

I thought Elena, who'd been to see Jano that afternoon, looked a bit gloomy. She was wearing a short, figure-hugging black dress. We danced and her body gave off a glow that mingled with that of the Pezinok wine inside me. I could detect her delicate odour and the smooth skin of her neck on my lips. My endorphins were working a treat.

"I'm dancing with the most beautiful culture rep in the whole of Slovakia," I whispered in her ear. She gave a melancholy smile. She raised her arms and put them round my neck and let me hold her even tighter to me. I could feel the softness of her breasts against my chest. There was nothing soft about any part of my own body.

As we left, all I could see was her. No matter that we were being watched. Even if that was by Jano.

Simples, a stroke of luck.

Aqua vitae

I woke around lunchtime. I had a thumping headache and my mouth was parched and tasted like a mixture of desert sand and sewage. I remembered getting up several times in the night to throw up. I glanced at the mirror and felt even worse. My eyes looked like embers that had just died.

"Look at you, you bright spark! You pride and *joy* of your family! You representative of the students of East Slovakia! You idiot…"

The third way of handling pain, a snapped-off thorn, a wound scratched raw? Hangover. Just a common-or-garden hangover.

There was nothing to be gained from further self-torment. My head was going to throb all day. I certainly didn't feel like eating.

Elena… I recalled. In some corner of a corridor she'd let me kiss her, but she never stopped gazing somewhere into the distance. Getting a hand inside her LBD had proved a bit tricky. She let me fret for a while, then grabbed me, looked me in the eyes and said:

"You're a good guy really, aren't you? Tell me you are."

"Me? Good? Why?" My hand was unwilling to cede the territory already conquered, struggled on for a while, but then reversed back out of the maze of folds, bits of elastic and zips. I lit a cigarette.

"Sorry," she said, "I'm sorry…" That 'sorry' sounded a bit odd: *I* was the one who should have been feeling guilty…

Then she told me how she spent the afternoon in Jano's room. For a private chat. I got through three or so cigarettes.

"You're a good guy really, aren't you? You are!" She kissed me, just a quick one.

"Sorry," … and she was gone.

Once I was back in bed my whole world went into a spin. Roast chicken, Očová, USCOS, Elena, cigarettes… I've no idea what followed… *Obscurum per obscurius* …

The others had already eaten when I arrived in the dining room after lunchtime. I ordered a coffee.

Then I suddenly spotted Solčáni, sitting at one of the tables. With Jano…

"Well good morning, sir! Listen. Comrade Lieutenant here has come to see you."

Solčáni was drinking coffee and smoking nervously. He was casually dressed, unshaven and, of all known detectives, probably put me most in mind of Columbo.

"You two know each other?" my surprise got the better of me, seeing them together, the officer who'd investigated Ľudka's murder and Jano – scrutineer of female cultural reps, supplier of farm produce and distributor of monies belonging to the Youth Union. In the card index of my life these two worlds were poles apart. Though actually – they did go together. Pain and treatment...

"Comrade Prcúch is an important witness himself. But it's you I've come to see," he said, glancing at Jano, who rose at once and left.

"Bad night?" he said, offering me a cigarette. I accepted. Surprisingly, I was able to smoke. Only my head was still throbbing away.

"The case is ninety-five per cent solved," he told me in his gravelly smoker's voice. "There's just a few details we still need. We're sure Ľudka knew her assailant."

"Really? Do you know who killed her?"

"I can't tell you that yet. But you mustn't let on to anyone!"

It felt as if I had an axe wedged in my brain. I could understand what he was saying, but it didn't make any sense.

"The letters you gave me in Košice were a great help. It was very good that I went to Košice," he said as if he was talking to himself. "Very good. It all fits perfectly."

He stubbed his cigarette out, stood up abruptly and left.

I suddenly realised I hadn't the foggiest idea why he'd come to see me.

And it was me he'd come to see, wasn't it?

Why wouldn't they leave me alone? She was dead, wasn't she?

I'm one small branch of your tree,
swaying here in the breeze.
"The tempest of revolution"
– writing this comes with such ease…

Tabula rasa!

I was back where wine tasted good. I was reciting my latest poem. The eyes of the female culture reps were twinkling with admiration.

"You should come to our club and give a recitation," a blonde from Nitra said. "We're setting up some poetry evenings. Will you come?"

Her name was Nina. Every time she said something, she leaned forward and grabbed my knee. She wasn't bad looking, but I'd never seen so many freckles on one face. So she probably wasn't a natural blonde. And she had tiny breasts, which was easy to verify during her regular grabbings of my knee. They were of that size dismissed as 'bee stings'.

"Yeah, poetry evenings, we have them as well," Hanka, a member of the Central Committee in Prague, joined in. "They're terribly important ideologically. Very nice little poem," she added, turning to me.

"You liked it? And do you know what it was about?"

"Obviously, the Party. I quite understand you."

"D'you know what I'd like to know?" I asked. "What the Party thinks about events like this course we're on."

She sat up. "Why?"

"Well, think about it. When you reckon that we flew all the way from the east of the country to Bratislava by plane, then there was the coach, then our board and lodging – a course like this for thirty people must cost quite a pretty penny. Then all we do here is a couple of hours pretending to listen to a lecture, followed by all the eating, drinking and other stuff…"

"I do understand what you're saying." She had to raise her voice because the DJ was starting another string of records. "But it can be quite important, meeting people, talking about issues, like us here, round this table. The Party needs young people to engage in a stream of activities that interest them and following that stream find a way to merge into one mighty river with the urban and rural proletariat and other workers, not excluding the intelligentsia."

"So in your view, I, having got totally pissed last night – had I done a good job for the benefit of the Party?"

She laughed and I went on: "Look… In all honesty, I'm having a whale of a time. I've met some interesting people, I've never stayed at a hotel like this, where I can go to the pool or the sauna whenever I feel like it, you could say I'm genuinely broadening my horizons… Yet I do feel slightly guilty. I'm a bit worried about going home to my family, friends, and colleagues at school and claiming to have had quite a tough time here building socialism."

"The bit about getting pissed, admittedly that wasn't exactly inevitable, was it… But for the rest, it's like I said. The building of socialism needn't always be gruelling. But I hear what you're saying and admit that some people don't quite get it."

"So might it not end in us losing our rapport with the masses?" I asked throwing my arms wide and slopping some of the wine out of my glass. "And another thing: might some of us not start thinking all this luxury is ours by right, something we deserve because of our status and importance?"

Nina of the tiny breasts and large freckles touched my knee and again presented me with a view of the *puszta*. "I think we're all due for a bit of quiet. What d'you reckon? Why don't we all go for a sauna?"

Well, at least we'd know whether you're a real blonde or not, I thought. I glanced towards Hanka. She had specs with thick lenses and about thirty kilos more than what she should have.

"Off you go then. My preference is for cool liquids. But I do understand."

The sauna was in the hotel basement. The communal changing room was deserted. Nina slipped her dress off and quickly shed her panties. I sat on a bench with my belt undone, gazing at that freckly puszta. Clearly she wasn't a true blonde. I experienced a brief dizzy spell.

She came across to me and started unbuttoning my shirt from behind. She stroked my chest. Her tiny breasts tickled me behind the ears. Having undone the last button her hand travelled on down over my lower abdomen, slipped neatly under my latex belt and seized her booty. Without letting go of it she came round to the front, knelt and gazed briefly, open-mouthed, as if she was filming me with her eyes. Then suddenly, like a hungry baby, she went to work. It took less than a minute.

I was still wearing my trousers. Not taking her eyes off me, she removed them. "Come on!" She grabbed my hand. Naked, we entered the sauna.

BARBA non fecit philosophum

Elena was there. In the dim reddish light, like when a camera flashes, I could see her wavy hair flowing across the thighs of the whiskered guy from the Centre. Černý. The nice guy. The poet. That good mate.

But now he looked anything but nice. Or poetic. Or friendly.

I turned: "Come away, let's not disturb them," I said to Nina.

"No, stay, both of you, don't go," Elena appeared to be pleading. Her voice was tinged with resignation and the vulgarity of ine-briation. I glanced at her again. She had a perfect body. Yesterday I'd held those breasts in my hands…

"Please, do come right in," she said.

"Are you okay?" I asked. "I haven't seen you all day."

"I've been…," she laughed hysterically, "…on a course… I've been being trained very thoroughly. My parents are going to be proud of me!"

Suddenly she began to sob. Her head started shaking and banging into Černý's member. Unlike the man himself it was enormous. I suddenly took against him. Not because of that long prick of his, but because of the cowed misery in her eyes. Because I'd seen that misery somewhere before, or I'd at least imagined it like this. Because I hadn't been able to forestall this cowed misery, because I hadn't protected what I should have protected.

"Come on, you need a good sleep," I said.

"Mind your own business, lad, okay?" Černý spoke at last.

"Can't you see she's not well, leave her alone!" I said, dragging Elena away.

"I suggest you stop playing the guardian angel. Look to your own floozy, okay?" He hauled Elena back and embraced her violently.

Suddenly I was quite sober. It was hot inside the sauna, but my voice was cold as ice.

"Right, let's be clear. You can be whatever you like, I couldn't care less. But you're not going to do any more harm to this lass." I pulled Elena, still sobbing quietly, to her feet. That prick loomed back into view, but not so long as before.

"And who are you? Timur and his team?" Černý sneered, twirling the end of his moustache between his fingers.

"I'm a Young Communist, just like you ..."

"Young Communist! Ha-bloody-ha! I'd better have you demoted to Pioneer!" he said.

I slammed the sauna door. I think Nina remained inside.

I wasn't bothered.

Beati
pauperes
spiritu

I've never slept well on trains. The couchettes are tailored to hobbits and the temperature is either ten degrees higher or ten degrees lower than it should be.

This time I was on my way to Bratislava to attend a training course for Youth Travel Agency guides. I was alone in my couchette compartment and spent the first couple of hours rolling over and back in the position of a crouched skeleton until I finally dozed off somewhere this side of Poprad. For about five minutes… At Poprad three men entered the compartment.

They switched on the light.

"Thur's some bloke sleepin' 'ere," said one of them.

"'S'all right, we'll keep t' noise down," said the second.

"So wur's that bottle o' borovička?" That was the third one, speaking like the other two in the broadest East Slovak dialect.

The bottle of Slovakian gin didn't last even as far as Štrba, their determination to 'keep t' noise down' not even that long.

"An' if yon minister thinks 'e can get away wi' it, well, we'll make 'im see 'e can't, an' that'll be that."

"We ain't gonna be fucked about by any arse'oles in Bratislava, oh no-o-o-o!"

"Unless they gi' us t' money for t' finishin' mill. Ďodi's workin' there now, so it should be possible to wangle summat… "

"No, Janči. Listen 'ere: The Tatras as a region need a distinct approach, and Comrade Minister 'as to get that into 'is thick 'ead!"

"But remember when he were 'ere last time round, what 'e told us in t' Koliba. Wait, Comrades, we are thinking about you… "

"All well an' good, but that were a year back and since then nowt, it's all soddin' Bratislava and bugger all for the East. Screw the lot of 'em!"

By the time Vrútky was behind us I'd had enough. "I'm going to fetch the attendant," I said.

"Arse'ole!" said one.

"All right, all right, we'll turn in now… We just needed to confer before tomorrow's meeting at the ministry," said the second.

"Who's 'e think 'e is … Our work's much more important socially, so you can shut the fuck up." That was number three.

By then I'd no hope of getting off to sleep.

"An' t' borovička, any good, is it?" I retorted.

"Oh, 's good all right. 'Ave some!"

At Žilina the train had a twenty-minute wait, just long enough to purchase a new half-litre bottle at the station buffet.

"And get some cheap fags while you're at it," they shouted after me from the carriage window.

Omnia mea mecum porto

The first group of Soviet tourists I acted as guide for came from Volgograd.

"First you have to get a few AT's under your belt, then I'll see how you've been doing and if okay, I'll find you the odd attractive PT," said Hanka, who headed up the tour guides section of the Youth Travel Agency in Prague. At my interview she'd recognised me at once.

"Well, well, look who it isn't! Welcome to the world of tourism! I know where you're coming from. Travel is the best way for the youth of the world to get to know one another and come together in a mighty international stream of solidarity and progress!"

AT was short for 'active tour(ism)', that is, receiving tourists from abroad, while PT meant 'passive tour(ism)', denoting trips abroad taken by citizens of Czechoslovakia. The vast majority of ATs were made up of Soviets.

The leader, aged about thirty, of my first incoming Soviet tour, was Olya, severe of countenance and powerful of handshake; she was a charge hand at some factory. Volodya, the ideologue of the group, had limpid, pale-blue eyes and always had a cigarette on the go. As soon as we took up residence in one of the spanking new hostels on Strahov Hill, he summoned me to his room.

"Kolya, fetch the suitcase!" he ordered, in Russian, one young lad with broad, heavy shoulders, a broad, pimply face and a broad smile that exposed two gold teeth. Kolya came back with a huge trunk, which Volodya opened to reveal some two hundred half-litre bottles of vodka.

"Come on, glasses, jump to it! May our tour be crowned with success!" he sent on in typically grandiloquent Russian. We lit up – fat *papirosa*s with their disposable cardboard tube for a mouthpiece. The glasses were refilled. Volodya and Kolya looked at me; I understood. A toast.

"To friendship!"

"Friendship!" they returned, laughing.

"We must teach you some proper Russian toasts!"

After the third round the bottle was empty and I made to go to my own room. *Shiroka strana moya rodnaya…* Volodya gave me two bottles to take with me. Kolya carried them for me. Russians know how to treat a chap.

I'd just started to unpack when there was a knock at the door. It was Olya.

"This is for you," and she handed me a bottle of vodka – now I had three. "We can share it. This evening, if you like…" Russians do know how to treat a chap. Especially the women.

Lunch consisted of pork schnitzels and potatoes; they asked for some bread to go with it. The waiters were clearly prepared; they had the bread ready. After lunch came the general instructions. "The main thing is to explain to them that toilet paper should be disposed of *in* the lavatory bowl, not somewhere next to it," as they'd kept stressing on our course.

"Toss your used paper in the toilet," I explained, in Russian.

"Of course, next to the toilet, right?" – that was Volodya.

"No, please put it down the toilet!" – me.

"Surely *not* down… Out of the question!" – Olya.

Me: "Drop it *down* the toilet!"

Volodya: "Right, we should drop it on the floor, yes? Understood, comrades?"

We took a Prague city tour. Wenceslas Square with the equestrian statue of Wenceslas IV, the 'father of the nation', the astronomical clock on Old Town Town Hall, from which the Czechs have a habit of tossing (dropping) those who have fallen out of favour, and round the corner the place where foreign rulers would cut out the tongues and cut off the heads of those who had fallen out of favour with them, and the Castle, seat of the President who did his damnedest to remain in good odour with all foreign rulers, and then in the evening to the Schweik Tavern, named after one who was apt to take the piss out of all of the above.

"Do you like Prague?" – Volodya and I were chatting, still in Russian, over pints of Pilsner Urquell.

"Oh, yes, a beautiful city. My uncle was here in sixty-eight."

"In sixty-eight, you say?" said the waiter, in Czech, as he plonked two more jars down in front of us, possibly a bit too aggressively, causing the head of foam to splatter: "On a tank, right?"

"*Da, da,* as part of a tank crew," Volodya replied. "He also liked Prague…"

The waiters were used to this kind of thing.

"Kolya, come on, fetch that case!" He rose to his feet and declared: *"There are two ways of knocking one back – thoughtfully and thoughtemptily. Let's be thoughtempty!"*

On the far wall of the restaurant hung impassively the fly-blown portrait of the Emperor Franz Joseph immortalised by Jaroslav Hašek, with its caption 'Take it easy!'. *Ad loc.*

Olya turned up just as I'd collapsed onto the bed. This time she didn't even bother to knock, just slipping silently in. Without a word she unscrewed the cap of the vodka she'd given me that morning and poured out two glasses.

"Down the hatch!" she said and tipped the contents of one glass straight down her shock-worker's gullet. She waited for me to follow suit then put out the light. That was the last thing she said.

As I lay there on my back, I could see her body, outlined against the window and rising and falling like the piston of a well-oiled engine. Her pudendum was going at it like a combine harvester scything through the black earth plains of Ukraine.

She was the second woman I'd had sex with. The first since Ľudka's death.

Vodka is a tried and tested Russian anaesthetic.

Genius loci

The whole next day was taken up with a coach trip.

At Terezín we saw the former concentration camp that had held Jews and political prisoners. I had some trouble interpreting everything into Russian. The elderly lady who was our guide and who claimed to be a survivor of the camp, told us a story about a group of young people who'd all been executed, a couple of days before the war ended, for being involved in organising the anti-fascist resistance in Bohemia.

Then it was off to Karlovy Vary, Carlsbad. All Soviet tour groups were taken there. (Which may be why so many ex-Soviets have come back since…)

I recalled our training course and the object lesson we'd be given about a certain guide: he was said to have explained to some Russian tourists that teabags, which they'd never seen before, were to be drunk by placing them in the mouth and imbibing hot water through them. Then he'd taken them for a walk along the promenade at Karlovy Vary, where – to the amusement of the entire town – little groups of Russians could be seen sipping hot, health-giving spa water from those typical Carslbad spa cups with a spout – with the tea bag string and tag dangling out of their mouths.

The guide had allegedly been dismissed on the instant.

Faber est quisque fortunae suae

After a tour of the spa complex and the porcelain works and a Becherovka tasting, they had an hour to fill at their leisure. They scuttled off to the shops and I lay myself down beneath the statue of Yuri Gagarin and tried to doze off.

"Are you asleep?" a girl's voice asked me in Russian.

"Yes," I replied ditto.

"Is it allowed to sleep next to monuments in your country?"

"And why not?" I unglued my eyes.

"Because it's disrespectful to the hero… At least that's our view. But you enjoy your lie-down if you want to. You do things differently here. I expect we've tired you out…"

"And you, why haven't you gone off shopping?"

"I like it here. I can't leave a spot like this – to go *shopping*! Just think what this man has achieved. Look at him! Born in a village in the middle of nowhere and now he's got a monument to himself, here, in a foreign land!"

I raised my head to look up at the metal monstrosity. Then I closed my eyes again.

"Back then he was only twenty-seven, and as he boarded the space ship he knew he might perish. He had a two-year-old daughter. Did you know that?"

I didn't.

"But he did board it, because someone had to, someone had to be the first and he was happy to be the one, and he knew that his life was a price worth paying. He flew in the face of death because that was the whole point of his life. If he hadn't gone and then lived to be a hundred, his life would have been worthless. And now, look, he's here, smiling, as if there was nothing to it…"

I sat up. She was a tiny, unassuming blonde. Behind her rather drab spectacles her vivacious eyes with a tinge of green wore a smile.

"It's like at Terezín," she said with a sigh. "I mean, it's so awful

47

that those young people didn't survive the war. Fancy dying just a couple of hours before the liberation! I can't believe it… All their friends and classmates who did nothing survived. They'd just been waiting for the war to end, for others to do things on their behalf. For others to die for them at the front – soldiers, partisans, resistance fighters. On our side, at Stalingrad alone, almost half a million soldiers died. Nine out of every ten fell during the first three days of the battle… Just imagine: in the evening they're playing cards, thinking of their girlfriends, their mothers. Ten of them. And next day…

"And then… then along come the ones who survive, and off they go – shopping."

"You're right," I said, "perhaps one shouldn't sleep on monuments. I've never given it any thought. Sorry!"

She had a lovely smile.

"What's your name?"

"Tanya."

"You never know, he might have been glad."

"Who?"

"Gagarin."

"Why? I don't follow."

"If you'd come down here, closer to me and if we'd lain here next to him together…"

Slowly the others started drifting back. At the feet of the first cosmonaut they set down their bags full of clothes, porcelain, sets of crystal glassware, and large carpets, each folded into a square.

Inter arma silent musae...

In the evening we went to see Chaikovsky's *Eugene Onegin* at the National Theatre.

We got there late. Loading all their shopping onto the coach had been as tricky as dragging a hedgehog out of a cage. Madame Larina and the nurse were already reminiscing about the old days. Our tickets were for the best seats in the front stalls. Thirty young Russian shock-workers in sweat-soaked Russian-style tunics passed between rows of Mozart's burghers of Prague in their dark suits and evening dress, blocking the latters' view of the idyllic Russian landscape on stage, complete with little birch trees. The peasantry began celebrating the harvest, singing merry songs, but it was plain that someone was going to kill someone. The last to come lumbering in were Kolya and Volodya, who'd hung back for a quick smoke.

On the coach back from the theatre Tanya and I sat together. For a long while neither of us spoke. I glanced at her – her eyes were brimming with tears.

"So sorry. I… it always gets to me like this… They're all so wretched… Olga, Lensky, Eugene and Tatyana." Her pale-green, dewy eyes were on me, full of trust. "Who do you think was the most wretched of all?"

"Tatyana?" I hazarded.

"Ah, Tatyana. Tatyana's so deeply in love… There's nothing wretched about that, even though she can't give her love away, but at least she has it for herself, it fills her whole being. And she's faithful and honourable and can be proud of herself…"

"Lensky?"

49

"Oh, yes, he has to die. He'll die in grief and the promise of his life will remain unfulfilled. But his death is brief, the pain transient. His life's been like the Springtime, lots of buds and lots of blossom. No, he isn't particularly wretched."

"Olga then."

"*Da*, Olga is truly wretched. She has eyes for herself alone and her awareness of her looks blinds her to her vacuous, egotistical self. Yet she doesn't know how to be wretched. To be able to be truly wretched, to know how to suffer, you have to see the poverty of your spirit, you have to grasp that you've spoiled everything you could, that anything you do will be a complete waste and bring only wretchedness to others. Eugene, yes, Eugene is most deserving of our compassion. He's simply beyond help," she sobbed into my shoulder.

Somehow or other we found ourselves in my room. She went on and on about birch groves, deep forests and lakes, the deep Russian soul, as wide open as the Russian landscape.

"Do you know any of our Russian songs?" she asked and at once began to sing. She closed her eyes, rose to her feet and started dancing. And at once it was as if she were not alone, as if, in that hostel room, a Russian village had sprung into life, gradually peopled by *muzhiks* and their womenfolk, all singing and dancing, and we two were bride and groom, she with colourful ribbons woven into her long blond plaits and I in my peasant blouse and white-embroidered linen trousers, and in my glorious, deep, pure bass I sang "Yaaaaaaaaaaaaaaaaay…" to my bride and time stood still and I was smiling a broad smile like Gagarin, the boy Yury from the next village, who'd just popped out into space for an hour or so, but had got back in time for our wedding.

The door opened and in strode Olya, the group leader. The plaits came undone, the ribbons faded, and the wedding guests ran off.

"Come on, off to your own room, bedtime, Tatyana," she said severely, and my bride left.

"I've brought you a present," she said, handing me a statuette wrapped in newspaper. It was a soldier armed with a machine gun, and it bore the legend "*Stand to the last!*".

"It's ours, the Stalingrad Monument. Let's have a drink," she said, handing me a glass even fuller than yesterday's.

In flagrante !

In the morning, Tanya came knocking.

"I'd like to give you a present," she said, handing me a statuette wrapped in newspaper. She spotted the selfsame statue from Olya on the table. "*Stand to the last!*"

She smiled sadly and the pale-green eyes behind her spectacles darkened a shade.

"Never mind, so you've got two presents the same. Yet they're not the same. One's true, the other's false. As in life – you have to choose."

She kissed me three times on the cheek and left.

That was our last shared morning. The group was heading off somewhere else. I saw them onto their train along with those bags full of clothes, porcelain, sets of crystal glassware and large carpets, each folded into a square. Before the train arrived, Volodya, Kolya and I, along with others, sat on their suitcases on the platform, smoking papirosas and making short work of several more bottles of Stolichnaya.

There are two ways of knocking one back – thoughtfully and thoughtemptily...

Shall we have one?

The train left, bearing away with it my sperm, which was doing its damnedest to fertilise the wrong egg.

*Ad
revidendum*

Anyone who is being nice to you, listening to you and showing a lively interest in your problems either needs something from you, or he's a queer. Kamil didn't need anything from me, nor, to the best of my knowledge, was he queer. At home he had a darkroom and an enlarger.

"Come round and bring all the negatives you've got. I'll do you some photos as a keepsake." That was about three months after Ľudka's death.

He lived in a lovely new house, part of a terrace built where some old houses had been cleared, not far from the city centre. All around there were tower blocks, but this street stood out, as if from another world. Quiet, cosy and … fit for a king. Kamil was an only child. In a separate room he had a vast model railway with Piko trains. As a boy I'd also had a few locos and carriages. And a boxful of track that I had to assemble every time I wanted to play with it, laying it all out over and over again on the living room carpet. I also had one level crossing, a bridge and two sets of light signals.

What Kamil had was an entire town, and when he switched the layout on, eight trains sprang into life, crossing barriers rose and fell, points changed, and the lights came on inside the tiny houses. Fabulous.

Then we went to eat. In the fridge he had csabai salami, pots of cod liver and jars of shellfish. He also produced a bottle of Cinzano bought at the Tuzex hard-currency shop. He showed me his holiday snaps. Spain, Yugoslavia, Cuba, Mexico... The countries' very names excited me...

Kamil and I had been friends since secondary school. He was always there anytime it mattered – at the cottage in the country the weekend Andy and I got drunk for the first time, on that skiing trip, even at the party at Mina's place, when we first learned how to kiss girls. Or not? Actually I'm not sure. He was certainly there, but I've no particular memory attached to him. I know who Boris, Ivan and Braňo were smooching with, I know Andrej described to us the ease with which he'd got inside Anka's blouse, which was subsequently confirmed by Braňo, who got so drunk that he fell asleep on top of Klaudia with his flies undone, and, since he weighed over a hundred kilos, she couldn't wriggle out from underneath him or wake him so she'd had to call for help, I know that Mina and I went out at midnight to get some cigarettes and managed to forget ourselves in a phone box and so missed Viera's striptease and so on, but where was Kamil and who was he with? He wasn't on the list of those who got drunk, or on the list of those caught *in flagrante*, or among those who were singing out on the balcony, or those who vomited into the neighbour's planter. So what was he up to there? What list was he on?

I can remember his shy smile, or rather grin, adopted so as to give no offense to anyone. He would keep an eye open for who needed what; his eyes generally had that special concerned expression in them usually seen in people who go to church, but Kamil didn't. But then who knows. At the time, officially nobody went to church.

And now too – after what had befallen me – not knowing how he might help, he'd come up with the photo thing. In the red light of the darkroom, each precious moment with Ľudka came floating up out of the developer. A trip to Budapest, a spring holiday at that country cottage, her performance with an ensemble at the Východná folklore festival, hiking in the Low Tatras… We must have done about a hundred. He wanted to keep some himself. Kamil was adept at enhancing the details of Ľudka's face and she looked back at me as if we'd been on that trip only yesterday.

Oh my God…

"Haven't you got any snaps of her from last year, when she was in Bratislava?"

No, I hadn't. From that last year I actually didn't have a single thing. We'd spent her last year each of us in a different place. And if ever we met, there was no time for taking pictures.

Kamil put all the photos in a large envelope. I didn't know

how to thank him.

"Don't mention it," he said with a grin.

The photos are all I have left of those three wonderful years. I've often looked through them. Which may explain why Ľudka's face keeps coming back to me when least expected.

I didn't see Kamil for a long time after that, only at class reunions, which he stopped coming to after the Velvet Revolution.

Instead, Boris once turned up with a list on which Kamil was…

Whenever someone's nice to you and shows a lively interest in your problems, there may be a third reason…

Amicus curiæ

And what of Corporal Huck?

He joined our company in Olomouc at the end of our boot camp. He was Czech, almost thirty and nearly missed being called up.

"Shit! They only remembered me at the very last minute; I was almost home and dry…"

Later, he would end such sentences with "… the commie bastards!" By then we'd become friends. "Listen, Doc, do you fancy some new trainers? The quartermaster's store has just had some in and they don't look bad."

Corporal Huck had flat feet and he'd been attached to the quartermaster. That apart, he was in charge of the commissary.

"I say, Doc, we've had a delivery of Hungarian salami. D'you want me to put one aside for you?""Doc, I need some leave of absence for the day, do me a chitty for hospital visit, will you? I've got a date in a hotel. You get the idea, I'll introduce you later…"

I don't remember his real name. Everybody called him Huck.

Huck Finn. Even the brass.

With several bottlesworth of premium Litovel coursing through our blood, we were coursing the streets of Olomouc by night, singing. Vilém from somewhere in the far west of Bohemia started roaring Karel Kryl's:

Bratříčku, nevzlykej, to nejsou bubáci, vždyť jsi už velikej, to jsou jen vojáci…

Koloman, a vet, joined in:

Ya nye sovyetskii, ya tolko russkii, ya peterburskii anarkhist…

The best of it was as we passed the Soviet barracks.

"They could lock us up for this, lads, and we'd never get out!" I tried to restrain them.

… menya zanyali, v Sibir poslali, patamu shto nye komunist! yodelled the artistic spirits of Dalibor, an architect, and Oliver, a musician.

"Look, Doc, I need to go to earth for a fortnight or so, I'm sick to the back teeth of army life. Commie bastards! Get me into the sick bay, say I've got the mange or something…"

Homo homini lupus est

Next day I took surgery as normal, though my stomach was playing up a bit. I think I was cutting some ARAB's ingrown nail and my hands were shaking.

"Fix me up with a chitty for a spa, will you, Doc? I could do with a spell at a spa."

The phone rang. "It's for you, Docture," said the medical orderly, aka scab-lifter, István, a Magyar, handing me the receiver.

"Come and see me at two o'clock in Pavilion IV, Comrade Doctor," – it was Major Krůta, the Czech head of counter-intelligence.

"Remind me later, István, I need to be on IV at two, *kérem szépen!*"

"*Persze*, Docture, at four on II, *biztos!*" He grinned. "*Vagy előléptetnek téged, vagy megbasznak.*"

Pavilion IV was in a remote corner of the barracks. It was a building like any other, except for the towering aerial on its roof.

"Thanks for coming, Comrade Sergeant," – here, in his world, I was no longer 'Doctor'. He was sitting at a solid, antique, non-army desk laden with files. He was scouring them for something, taking his time… Then he glanced sharply up at me.

"I'll get straight to the point. I've had a good look at your file and I'm in no doubt at all that you care about the wellbeing of our socialist motherland. The sick bay is a place where you en-counter various kinds of people, which gives you the chance to be on friendly terms without regard to status or rank. You must be on your guard and keep your ears open. It has come to our notice that something is stirring in the officer corps. Various things are being said there that could jeopardise the foundations of military discipline and our readiness to confront the enemy.

"Keep a particular eye on Captain Kopáč. I gather that you and he are on friendly terms. Stay that way, but be vigilant. And alert. I'm sure you understand what is expected of you.

"And as for the…," he checked me as I was making my way out through the door, "… as for that rowdy singing in the street, I trust you'll come to your senses, Comrade Sergeant."

Vagy előléptetnek téged, vagy megbasznak. Either you're up for promotion, or you're in for a bollocking.

Imperium!
in imperio

Kopáč was a *politruk* and ran the literature and theatre circle.

"Right, let's get to it, lads, ideas please! What shall we do?"

There were about ten of us, tender souls in search of an island of civilisation amid the sea of green, or at least a cushy something into which to escape. The circle was called 'Inter Arma'.

Kopáč handed round cigarettes.

Ľuboš Lejko, a thin blond guy from Stará Ľubovňa, raised his hand.

"You've got something?" Kopáč asked.

Ľuboš took a tiny little book from his pocket. Jacques Prévert, *Words*.

The zip slid down the small of your back
and all the happy storm of your passionate body
submerged in darkness
burst suddenly
And your dress dropping on to the polished parquet
made no more sound
than an orange peel dropping on carpet
But under our feet
its little pearl buttons crackled like pips
Blood orange
lovely fruit
the tip of your breast
has traced a new line of fortune
in the palm of my hand
Blood orange

lovely fruit
Sun in the night.

"That's very nice, Private. Best kept for the Bechyně armed forces amateur dramatics festival. We here, as 'Inter Arma', we should be rehearsing something that'll demonstrate our ideological maturity, the moral edge we have over our imperialist enemies. Has anyone else got anything?"

Silence.

Huck took a drag on his cigarette. "We could do some Seifert…"

Kopáč shot him a glance but said nothing.

"Suppose we recite some Válek?" I suggested. His *Word*. We did it as a student drama thing. It's good."

"Excellent, Doc. But we really ought to add something Soviet as well. Or at least Russian."

"We could give 'em Ruslan and Ludmila," Huck grunted.

"You know, that's not a totally crazy idea. Who can remember what it's about?"

"*Persze hogy pamätám.* Puskin Sándor?" the scab-lifter, István, ventured.

The following week Kopáč brought the text along and shared out the parts. I was Ruslan and my Ludmila was Ľuboš. Koloman played the evil dwarf Chernomor, who carried my bride off. He was aided by Vilém as the seductive and treacherous Naina. István played all the Pechenegs. He was given a child's rocking horse and with his accent and magyarised Slovak he was quite the part. The Pechenegs attacked Kiev and István skipped all over the stage on his horse shouting "*Talpra Magyar, hí a haza!*"

until the heroic Ruslan arrived. Huck was given the part of the kindly sorcerer Finn. It was actually from then that we'd called him that, he having refused to be any kind of Russky.

"If Finn, then Huckleberry, Huckleberry Finn. I quite like him. He's a rebel, added to which he's American!"

So we did Válek and Pushkin. Every Friday evening, from seven till nine. *Castigat ridendo mores*

All in all it was quite a frolic. Sort of like a wedding at the Kievan court of Prince Vladimir the Bright Sun. It was easy to drum up the extras among the troops, with one who could juggle, another who could do somersaults, while Oto and Dežo from the first platoon were brilliant at break dancing. The lads even formed pairs and danced a *khorovod*, a Russian girls' round dance. Oliver played the piano, composing the music himself, and it was simply fantastic. As heady as Russian perfume, but also jaunty and inexhaustible like a Cossack dance. We had balloons, coloured lights and soap bubbles everywhere. Prince Bright Sun was dazzling. We even had a Great Head, cleverly contrived from cardboard boxes glued together by Dalibor, he of the architecture degree. It was perched against the backdrop, wearing a severe expression and guarded by two camo-suited soldiers holding machine guns; goodness knows how Kopáč had managed to get them issued for such an event. My Ludmila in her Russian folk costume and a blond wig was a sight for sore eyes. They were almost rolling in the aisles when I declared my love to her and she, with the lights dimmed, made as if to undress for our wedding night. Then just the two of us were left on stage with the Great Head at the back.

Dramatic music from the piano. Then in came Chernomor to envelope the naked Ludmila in his voluminous beard and bear her away.

> *Horror – the girl he loved had gone!*
> *Ruslan clutched at the empty air;*
> *the shadows yielded no Lyudmila,*
> *a force unknown had snatched her off.*
> *My friends, if one of you's a martyr*
> *to love and suffers hopelessly,*
> *he'll live a wretched life, it's true;*
> *he will live, though, you may be sure.*
> *But what if after long, long years*
> *you've now at last embraced your sweetheart –*
> *the one you've yearned for, pined for, wept for –*
> *then, at the moment of your union,*
> *you lose her for ever – oh, my friends,*
> *myself, I'd sooner die than that!*

Except I didn't die. I was quite a hunk, a Russian champion, and since I was suddenly free, all manner of beauties set about seducing me, the director having gone to particular trouble with that bit, especially over the costumes and make-up. Friends who we only ever saw in camo suits and combat boots and with their heads shaved were transformed into bewitching, ethereal beings, so that certain sex-starved comrades in arms in the audience had trouble knowing what to do with their hands, as if the garrison were enjoying a visit from Marlene Dietrich or Lady Diana.

I was also quite taken with the beautiful witch Naina, but Ruslan was unaffected by her and went off in search of Ludmila.

My first battle was with the Great Head. That was where Válek first came into it. I pondered my own self:

And to whom do I owe the person I am?
The Communist Party, which taught me how to become a man?

I grabbed a huge sword and hacked away at that gigantic, glowering face until it begged for mercy.

You brought me to my senses,
valiant hero…

Then I did battle with Chernomor. Once more I drew my warrior's sword and roared at him together with Válek:

Those card-carrying swindlers can go to hell!

And I sliced his long beard right off. Everyone was jubilant, they sang and danced, but they still had to liberate the city from the Pechenegs. So I harried István on his rocking horse, cut off his head, and the party could go on. But I still hadn't got Ludmila, because she was under a spell, and only when Finn gave me the ring with which to bring her round could we be re-united.

I contributed a poem of my own to the script.

How oft has a Pecheneg set foot here – so cruel
How many Great Heads have tried to tell us
How to live and What to think
How many dwarfs have smeared their beards in our gruel
And they're become the missing link!?

Cut the empty twaddle!
History already has too much on tick
For too long now so many feckless idlers
Have taken charge and played the bolshevik
No, the cure for tyranny isn't tenderness.

Despite th' allure of all those nymphs beguiling
Dear beloved hero, my defender
For the freedom of our sweet Ludmila
The necks of Head, and Dwarf, and Pecheneg to sunder
Be thy sharp sword their killer.

It was quite something!   *Est modus in rebus*

"Aren't you the subversive, eh, Doc?" said Corporal Huck Finn. "Not bad, that, asking *to whom do I owe the person I am?* It's obvious you owe it to those commie bastards! Nice one, Doc, you really pulled something off there!"

Koloman the vet brought some pork loin from the AAU (Auxiliary Agrarian Unit), the farm he would invariably go to check on whenever they had a pig-slaughtering. The oil warming on the two-ring mini-hob sputtered quietly, the whole sick-bay was bathed in the smell of fresh pork. István the scab-lifter did the steaks à la *lacipecsenye* and conjured up a bottle of apricot brandy to go with them.

"*Egészségünkre*, chin-chin, Docture!"

Dalibor slid his empty glass forward: "Long live our noble Prince Bright Sun! Long live our beautiful Princess Ludmila!"

"Down with Great Head!" cried Vilém. "Death to Chernomor!"

"Send the Pechenegs back beyond the Urals! And the Magyars beyond the Danube!" echoed Koloman.

"Stick the Czech in a sack and toss the sack in the Danube!" said Huck, quoting the popular Slovak dictum with a smile.

"I'm not givin' you any, Kálmán, you anti-Magyar wotsit, er.., element!" said István, refusing to pour a glass for Koloman.

"*You brought me to my senses, valiant hero…* I'm sure you know what I meant…"

"We're all Pechenegs," Oliver observed. "When they came here from Asia, they interbred with the locals. If they were willing, fine, if not, then by force. But you know what Slovak girls are like. They'd unroll a sheet of turf and that was that. Consequently there's a bit of Pecheneg DNA in all of us."

"And are Pechenegs the same thing as Magyars?"

"Shit! So I'm actually a Magyar…," Koloman concluded tragically.

"Better than being a bloody Russian," Huck couldn't resist adding.

"See, *barátom*, we're friends. *Fele Magyar, fele Tóth*, Hoongarian, Slovak, half an' half. Here, have a snifter. Pyoor Hoongarian firewater. *Még egy lacipecsenyet?*"

"Thank you, Lacipecheneg!"

Thereafter we called him Lacipecheneg. I think it's a brilliant name for a Magyar scab-lifter in the service of the Czechoslovak People's Army.

"Hey, Lacipecheneg, give us a bit more o' that brandy. Your doc here is an even bigger subversive than we thought!"

"You know what, guys? I've got a feeling we've proved we really do have that moral edge!" Dalibor wound up the debate.

Qui tacet consentire videtur . . .

That night a state of emergency was declared in Poland. With Lech Wałęsa at its helm, Solidarity was threatening the very foundations of the socialist system.

"Jaruzelski fixed it so the Russkies wouldn't come in like they did in Czechoslovakia in sixty-eight," said Corporal Huck.

We were placed on alert. All leave was cancelled. No going out on the town, no passes to leave the base.

Lieutenant Colonel Vančík was the chief political commissar. We were treated to a pep talk, in Czech, on Marxism-Leninism. The only military activity I ever had to take part in, doctor or no.

"Comrades, men! Our brothers in the Polish People's Republic are living through difficult times. Under the pretext of organising labour unions the enemy has presumed to disrupt the building of communism in our fraternal neighbouring country. We cannot stand idly by and watch as agents of western imperialism seek to destroy all that the Polish people have achieved during the thirty-five years since the Second World War in cooperation with the Soviet Union and their other true friends, including socialist Czechoslovakia. Our message to doubters is: Alliance with our Polish comrades is the guarantee that genuine solidarity will prevail. And if the need arises, we are ready to reciprocate the aid which the Polish army brought to us when this country needed it in 1968. Just as Polish soldiers, shoulder to shoulder with the glorious Red Army and the other armies of the Warsaw Pact, helped to safeguard the socialist system in our beloved motherland, so are we prepared at any time to safeguard socialism in Poland! Any questions?"

The silence was broken only by a fit of smoker's coughing from Corporal Huck.

"Yes, Corporal?"

"Erm, I just," he coughed again, "I'm sure the Poles don't want us turning up the way they did here in sixty-eight."

Lt Col Vančík adjusted his spectacles. Now it was his turn to cough.

"Corporal! The workers of Poland wish to work in peace. The workers of Poland trust their Party, and the workers of Poland know that if the worst comes to the worst they can rely on their friends in the Soviet Union and the other states of the Warsaw Pact. Any further questions, Corporal?"

"But we've no way of knowing. Our workers didn't welcome the armies of the Warsaw Pact with open arms either…"

To leave the barracks during a state of combat readiness was extremely risky. It counted as desertion, punishable by firing squad during an actual war, and now, in peacetime, by three or four weeks of close confinement, if not actual incarceration at the notorious military prison in Sabinov.

Lieutenant Colonel Vančík had a beautiful wife, twenty years his junior. The previous medic was said to have made a habit of paying her a visit whenever Vančík was on duty. And Vančík was said to be inordinately jealous. One night, while he was acting duty officer for the unit, he popped home to check on his wife. My colleague just managed to escape via the balcony and Vančík received a party reprimand for leaving the garrison. Rumour had it that he had entered his flat with his gun loaded and primed…

That made visiting and humping Comrade Mrs Vančík even riskier.

Monika.

I knew her as a patient. Vančík had brought her to the surgery one time, with a pricking pain near her heart. I examined her with particular care, including a meticulous auscultation and thorough palpation of her chest, exactly as the textbook demands. "To avoid misdiagnosis and leave nothing to neglect, it is vital that the patient be examined in an undressed state," Professor Takáč used to insist. I paid special attention to her heart sounds at the second and fifth intercostal spaces.

She didn't so much as blink. By contrast Vančík, standing behind her, kept clearing his throat nervously as he eyed my every move. As I took her blood, sitting opposite her on a chair with our knees touching, his eyes x-rayed my crotch, for all that it was masked by my doctor's gown.

"I'll give you a call when I get the results back," I said.

I had her home phone number on file.

Parturient montes, nascetur ridiculus mus...

Monika Vančík had a lovely face, but otherwise the whole event is barely worth recalling. Things went all too smoothly. Corporal Finn, who was on duty at the gate, failed to spot me leaving the barracks and as I came back in he just winked. Lieutenant Colonel Vančík didn't leave the barracks and didn't turn up to blow my head off. The children in the next room didn't wake up to come and stand in the doorway and gaze bleary-eyed at the Baroque spectacle we presented. Monika spread her legs so wide that inside her cave I felt like a bat lost in the Domica Cavern concert hall. I flittered about inside her for, so far as I can guess, under three minutes, probably even less. Instinct has always told me that the woman has to be satisfied, but I abandoned that notion at once in Monika's case. She let out no sound, whether sigh or groan, only a squelching noise down between her legs whenever something moved in that region, whether my penis, hand or tongue. The taste of old onions wasn't drowned out even by her strong perfume, which reeked of lily-of-the-valley.

But I was a soldier and I had completed my mission. I muttered something as I did up my army tie and quickly made myself scarce. I hawked and expectorated my way back to the barracks through night-time Olomouc and could taste the onion-flavoured lilies-of-the-valley for the next two days.

On the one occasion in history when the Czechoslovak People's Army might have been deployed I'd been having it off with the wife of the political commissar.

I felt lousy.

Requiescat in pace!

Jaruzelski mastered the situation in Poland and we didn't have to go there. That night I was the only soldier who'd been deployed.

Yet one shot *was* fired. Just before dawn actually.

Ľuboš Lejko, the slim fair-haired guy from Stará Ľubovňa who'd recited Prévert, put a bullet through his brain while on guard duty. He'd been due to go on leave, but had had it cancelled because of Poland. His friends in signals said that he'd phoned his girlfriend the night before.

"He also asked to see you, Doc."

When I was called to him, he had his machine gun in one hand and Prévert's *Words* in the other.

As a doctor I was superfluous.

Thanks, Ľuboš, for not doing it a couple of hours earlier. Otherwise I'd have been up shit creek with you.

"Come on, Doc, you could do with a snifter," said Captain Kopáč, taking me by the shoulder, once Private Lejko's body had been taken away by ambulance. It was like a rag doll in mud-spattered fatigues that were too big for him, with huge combat boots at one end and a mushy red mess at the other. Ruslan's Ludmila, fragile, vulnerable, pulverised, defeated.

Kopáč led me into the political section and fished a bottle of whisky out from behind the collected works of Lenin.

"You'll have to do the paperwork," he said as he handed me a brimful jar that had once contained mustard.

"Then you and Vančík will have to go and tell the parents. And you must give them this…"

The volume of Prévert's verse. *Words*. Well thumbed, dog-eared, and read a thousand times by torchlight in his sleeping bag, now freshly smudged with mud and blood.

As he was passing it across to me it flew out of his hand and floated off through space. It glided over the Captain's desk, hovered briefly above a bust of Lenin as if for a quick chat, then it paid its respects to the portraits of Gottwald and Husák on the wall and slowly sailed past the bookcases as if looking for a niche. It read the authors' names, the books' titles and couldn't make up its mind. It seemed pleased that some of the books were bound in red, like itself. Quietly it tucked itself away among them. So quietly that the layer of dust barely even eddied with the last wave of its wings.

Then the dust began to settle on the fresh, still wet blood.

Oh Barbara
What shit stupidity the war
Now what's become of you
Under this iron rain
Of fire and steel and blood
And he who held you in his arms
Amorously
Is he dead and gone or still so much alive
Oh Barbara   *Pro Patria*

We made the trip to Stará Ľubovňa in the official Tatra 613.

"Have something with you to help calm the parents down, Doc. You can give them a jab the minute we get there." I'd already got my first aid bag ready, including some parenteral diazepam.

Vančík sat next to the driver, the proper place for the officer in charge. The entire journey passed in silence.

The Lejkos lived on the second floor of a tower block. We rang the bell. Mrs Lejko came out onto the balcony. When she saw us she screamed.

I can hear that shriek to this day.

"What's happened? Where's Ľuboš, where's my dear Ľuboš?" she cried.

"I'm afraid we have some bad news, ma'am. May we come inside?" said Lieutenant Colonel Vančík.

Paralysed with pain, she stopped screaming and obediently went back inside. In a moment she had come down and opened the gate.

"Your boy is dead, ma'am. He died this morning. On guard duty."

I gave her a subcutaneous shot in the arm while we were still on the stairs; she offered no resistance, as if she hadn't even noticed. She still hadn't said a word. She just looked at us, first one, then the other, emissaries of death.

"Where's the boy's father?" Vančík asked.

"He's… he's not in…," she whispered.

"Ľuboš…," I began, "Ľuboš took his own life," and I took her by the hand. "He shot himself. I expect he was feeling low…"

She looked at me. She didn't seem surprised. Life began returning to her eyes. I couldn't be sure whether she was looking to me for help, or at me as a target.

"Why did you take him from me?" she wailed. "Why did you take him from me?" She turned to the man in command. "What did you need him for? He'd never hurt a soul, neither man nor beast. What did you need a soldier like that for? What for?" She lapsed back into silence.

"I was Ľuboš's friend," I said. "I know what a good lad he was. He would often recite to us from this book," and I handed Prévert's poems to her. I'd cleaned off the blood and mud.

She took the book in her hands, bursting into tears for the first time.

"Why didn't you help him? You're a doctor… a doctor, aren't you? You had to know he'd never make a soldier. Why couldn't you have given him a note and have him sent home? Home…!"

I put an arm round her.

Should I have told her that Ľuboš had been looking for me the night before? That he'd wanted a word? That if he'd found me, if I hadn't fucking well been… That perhaps…?

"I know what you're feeling," I heard myself say instead. "I know there are no words that can bring you any comfort."

"You know nothing, Doctor! How can you say any such thing! You can't know how a mother feels who only ten minutes ago had a son, and now she has no one…"

I hated myself. I hated being a doctor, I hated the army, I hated having to be the bearer of such tidings while wearing the aspect of a saviour, I hated her needing to hug me, to cast herself upon my factitious embrace, I hated my hypocritical words, I hated the way they made this abandoned and bereft, suffering woman seek support, hope, solace from me.

"I know, I do know, dear woman," my voice went on. "I too have lost someone close to me," – and it was out. The basest of all weapons had been unsheathed. "Someone killed my fiancée when she was only nineteen…"

At first her tears were heartrending, then they grew more subdued until the final sob went right through her frame. My own tears seeped unobserved into her hair.

"Let me make you some tea at least," she said.

Morituri te salutant

The disco at the club had been organised by Jano Prcúch. Ľudka had only popped in for a short while, being packed and ready to leave for Košice. Her train had been due to leave at midnight.

It was a fine summer's night and the student residence was awash with hormones.

Afterwards someone told me how beautiful she'd looked, with a fresh tan, happy. She couldn't wait to see me the following day. Everyone wanted to dance with her. She only chose people she knew. Her last nice time, last nice words.

She turned down the arrogant lads at the bar. She didn't like being spoken to as if she was the speaker's property.

Then she went up to her room to collect her bag, and on the way to the stop to catch a bus to the station, a car without headlights pulled up alongside her.

They pulled her inside. Someone poured some wine down her throat. She begged them, she'd miss her train, they could drop her at the station. "Why go all the way to Košice when you can have fun with us here?"

She was too pretty to be allowed to leave.
She was too good to make them happy.
She was too honest to be allowed to live.

Beatae memoriae...

I can't recall now whether the pub Vančík and I found was right there in Stará Ľubovňa, or somewhere in the Pieniny, where the sheer beauty and purity of Nature stripped us of our grief, or whether it was up in the Tatra Mountains, where we might remind ourselves of our insignificance and ridicule our dirty little secrets, or in Liptov, where courageous and simple folk still live, such good people in whose company we're not ashamed to speak the truth.

"You did well, Doc," Vančík said. "Really well." To start us off he bought a couple of large borovičkas and some beer.

"Listen, that girl of yours... Did someone really kill her?"

"Yes, Comrade Lieutenant Colonel. They did, you'll know the case," and I reminded him of what the television and newspapers had been full of five years previously.

"Oh, yes, the student girl, I remember... And who did murder her?"

"Apparently a bunch of yobs. Seven of them. The investigation's only just been completed, and the case is coming to court quite soon..."

"When?"

"Two weeks' time, in Bratislava, Comrade Lieutenant Colonel."

He became lost in thought.

"That must have been terrible... They should hang 'em. Or shoot 'em. Or both! Come on, Doc, let's have another. And call me Antonín, will you?"

His eyes were shining. "Tell me, Doc, how did you cope, it must have been terrible," he repeated. "I expect you loved her a lot, right...?"

I lacked the strength to contemplate this entire situation. All I wanted to do was drink. Vančík wouldn't let me order anything; he just went on getting in one round after another himself.

"But I'll tell you this much, Doc. Love, love is the direst misfortune. Love is like a nightingale that changes into a vulture and pecks away at your flesh while you're still alive. Count your blessings that yours will remain in your memory as a nightingale …"

I recalled Monika Vančík's vast rear end, which I'd given a working-over something after midnight. Lilies-of-the-valley, onions. I suddenly felt sorry for the Lieutenant Colonel.

Yes, I had a strong urge to tell him the truth. The truth as pure as the tear in the corner of his eye. Comrade Lieutenant Colonel, Antonín, mate, last night I fucked your wife. Last night I fucked your entire bloody army, that whole masquerade, the charade of discipline, the battle readiness, you're not going to believe this, Antonín, but we've got one political commissar, the most shiney-arsed ARAB you ever did see, he gives us our pep talks on Marxism-Leninism, well, you should just hear the man and you wouldn't know whether to laugh or start throwing up. Puking, that's the word for it, puking. Anyway, I shagged this ARAB's wife, silly tart – and she *is* a tart, she's fit to make me puke as well, but I shagged her anyway to show him how puny, how ridiculous he is, him and his whole shitty army. I did it to avenge all those Private Lejkos and all my other mates who have to jerk off in their quarters with twenty beds to a dorm while their sex-starved girlfriends are waiting for them back home … I did it for all of us who have to pretend we're thrilled to be on military service, and if we're convincing enough you'll let us out for four hours so as to forget about our girlfriends, or for two days so as to find out that our girlfriends have forgotten about us...

"Your wife, Comrade Lieutenant Colonel," I said instead, "is positively charming." He flashed a quizzical glance my way and then chuckled. We clinked our beer glasses and filled the entire pub with peals of laughter.

"A nightingale become vulture! A devil with the face of an angel – if you'll permit a political officer to use such language, ha ha ha... But you won't say I said so, will you, Doc..."

In vino veritas

My revenge had been pointless. To no effect. I had spilled my seed in vain. I had risked my life and venereal disease just to shag an empty balloon.

The lieutenant colonel went on with his zoological-theological tirade. I said nothing. I supped my beer and thought of my own dead nightingale and of Ľuboš, my second Ludmila.

"D'you know what, Comrade Lieutenant Colonel?"

"Do call me Antonín, okay, Doc?"

"Right, Antonín, d'you know what?"

"No, Doc, I don't..."

"All right, I'll tell you. D'you actually know who killed my Ľudmila?"

"But Doc, you said..."

"Bollocks, Antonín, bollocks! I'll tell you, but shhhh! It's top secret! Ľudmila was killed by the Great Head!"

Antonín gulped.

"Great Head? Meaning who, Doc?"

"I can't tell you that, Antonín. Nobody knows. But you might be able to find it in your books."

"What books?"

"Obviously, those… your ones…"

"You mean… ?"

"Yes, Comrade Lieutenant Colonel, I do!"

"Hang on, Doc, you mean… Marx, Lenin and the like?"

I nodded and downed my last glass. In the political commissar's tired and distracted eyes there was the briefest flash of suspicion like the last soldier of a surrendering army.

"Come on now, who reads Marx and Lenin in this day and age?" He stared into the bottom of his beer glass, then knocked back his empty shot glass. He raised his head and glanced at me. He looked like someone who'd managed to drop his trousers in a public park in the nick of time, rejoicing at not having shat himself and expecting the passers-by to share his *joy*.

"So, Great Head, you say. You know what, Doc?"

"No, Antonín, no I don't."

"You could be right about that Head…"

And after a pause he added:

"You know what, Doc? You're gonna go to Bratislava for the trial!"

"Come off it, Antonín!"

"You're going. That's an order!"

Right then…

I absolutely wanted to see their faces. More than five years had passed and now something akin to satisfaction was imminent. The execution of justice.

The frisk search at the Palace of Justice was perfunctory. If I'd wanted to, I could have easily smuggled a knife in, perhaps even a gun.

"We don't want any trouble," the cop said as he patted me down. "Anyone taking it into their head to carry out their own form of justice…"

I had a sense that he wouldn't have minded if they did.

But how many would I have time to slice the prick or shoot the balls off before they stopped me? One? Two?

There were seven of them… I watched them being led along the old, tiled corridor. I had them at arm's length. I could see into their eyes.

I felt nothing.

I'd often imagined tracking them down somehow, luring them to some secret spot where we wouldn't be found and torturing them until they told me exactly what had happened. All I wanted was to know the truth. Now I was hearing it. The prosecutor read out the charges. Everything slotted together. The disco, kidnap, orgy, rape, murder. I was waiting to see if the story might not end differently. Whenever I'd heard, read or thought about that evening, I'd always hoped against hope that it would end differently. That at the last minute they'd have second thoughts. That the one who drew the short straw would suddenly say, come on, lads, let's not do anything stupid, she's a lovely girl, let's all just go home, this is ridiculous. That they'd wrap her in a blanket and drive her back to the hostel. Or that they'd leave her there by the lake, naked and hurt, but alive at least… Or that they'd cut her tongue out, erase her memory, disfigure her face, but let her live.

Let her come back to me. I would have made her well, I would have loved her even more, I wanted nothing more…

They'd raped her a second time. Out there by the lake. Just before they pushed her head under water.

What time could it have been – three, four in the morning? How much can a person suffer in four hours? How long does it take to lose consciousness under water? When had she stopped being L'udka and become just a body, a conglomeration of cells, suffocating organelles, whose existence is counted out by the passing minutes? With no hope of turning back, being a person again.

The prosecutor sought the death penalty all round. Of course, how could it be otherwise?

How otherwise?

After the sentence was read out, some woman started screeching. She ran up and down the corridor of the Palace of Justice in despair, crashing into the walls, tearing at her hair, throwing herself on the ground. For a moment it looked as if she was having an epileptic fit, then as if she was deranged or drunk. She kept babbling something unintelligible, then she started howling, louder and louder until she reached a high throaty pitch that was positively ear-splitting. People formed a circle around her and stared. She ran round and round the circle, rolling about on the floor and crashing into the onlookers. Suddenly she was at my feet. She entwined my legs in her arms, sobbing. Slowly she raised her head, her greasy hair with its grey roots showing parted to reveal her deep, black eyes. They were filled with pain and hate. She still had her arms about my legs.

"She's alive. Do you hear? She's alive!" she hissed so that only I could hear. "I've seen her. She was here this morning. She's alive! Go and find her! Understand? Go and find her!"

Two policemen came over, seized her under the arms and dragged her off. She was still screaming something unintelligible.

She's the mother of one of the murderers, people around me said. The worst one's. The one who got twenty-four years.

I had to get back to the barracks.

Si tecnisses philosophus mansisses!

"D'you know, Corporal, our Vančík isn't really such a bastard?"

I was having a drink with the lads on the last evening before our return to civvy street.

"Yes, Doc, I know. Basically no one's really a bastard, some just act the swine now and again. The real bitch of it is when someone acts the swine when there's no need. The thing is that we shouldn't ever have to be ashamed of anything we've done, Doc…"

He looked at me, his jolly moustache white with beer froth, but his eyes were deep and sorrowful.

On the way back to barracks we sang our heads off; the whole of Olomouc must have heard us. We put heart and soul into it especially beneath the windows of the Soviet garrison.

Run away home, Ivan,
Natasha's waiting for you,
run away home, Ivan,
and don't come back again!

At the barracks it was Kopáč on duty. "Come on, Corporal, let's go and say good-bye to the duty officer."

"Right you are, Doc."

"Well, well, lads, you're not interested in going home tomorrow? That's easy to arrange. If you want, I can always put you on fourteen days jankers," he said, grinning. He gave us each a cigarette.

"Captain," I said gravely, or as gravely as my liquid intake permitted. "We're off 'ome tomorrow and you're stayin' here. What a bugger! The Corporal 'ere's just been sayin' as we shouldn't be ashamed of anythin' we've done. An' I agree wi' 'im."

"All right, lads, all right...," the duty officer sought to console me.

"But there's somethin' else I need to say," I wasn't going to be put off. "It's just as important that we shouldn't be ashamed of anythin' we 'aven't done either. Anyway... In a nutshell I just wanted to thank you for not bein' an ARAB, it's thanks to you we've managed to survive."

I took a beer mat out of my pocket – I'd filched it in the pub – and slid it under the lapel of his uniform jacket. He already had some bits of chest candy there.

We hugged, his yellow lanyard scraped the skin on my face. Tottering, we saluted. "Good luck, lads!"

"One more thing, Captain. I'm not sure if you know or not, but watch yourself. Krůta's on your case."

He stood stock still, open-mouthed, and the good-natured wrinkles that formed whenever he laughed gradually smoothed away.

"Shit, Doc, that's buggered it," said Corporal Huck.

Quoad vitam

She really was alive.

She would come and see me. Irregularly, unpredictably, unannounced. She was suddenly there.

I'd never been any good at drawing, I had no photographic memory, but her face – it wasn't a memory, a lacklustre, smudgy image, it was a living being. I could study its every detail, discovering details previously unobserved, the gently compressed corners of her mouth, the wisp of hair above one ear, the sublime arc of her cheeks. It was she. Except that she didn't speak. She never said a single word. Just watched with her dark green eyes. It did seem sometimes that she was trying to say something. Something pressing, urgent, as if she needed to get me to do something, though I had no idea, no inkling what. But when all's said and done she was dead and this was a pure chimera, a by-product of the electrical activity going on within my brain.

I often dreamed that she was alive. But we never got to talk. People came to tell me she was alive, that she'd come back. Though she never came back to me. I was glad she was alive and looked forward impatiently to when we would meet; I wanted to be, to live with her. But she needed to recover, and as time passed it looked as if she was putting me to the test: Was I deserving of her return to me?

Or was she afraid I might not want her back?

You know what it's like: you wake up and for a brief instant you don't quite know what's what. Time and again I had to relive the painful process of accepting the true state of affairs.

I wrote a poem.

... and then women began showing me their breasts
and the stench of my boyhood beds
changed into a very bower of bliss
and the flames shooting from my torrid bosom
bore to the heights
the sooty deposits of my childhood.
(With Eva) went the igloo by the railway beyond the town
(With Darina) the clapped-out bicycle
not like any made today
and the marbles with all those ways of flicking and getting them
nicked by big boys
the games of hide-and-seek and ball-tag
daring voyages upstream

top marks and chocolate from Mum
and Dad's fairy-tales whenever I was ill.
A then when childhood died
and I was born
then here and there among the soot for a second or two
a ray of green shone through
a ray of perfect mid-teens happiness.
In its light I saw a boundless landscape
full of love – the unploughed field
that beneath my hands would bring forth
abundance from then till the death
that never crossed my mind…

Ah, Ľudka…
Ľudka…
Forgive my breaking in on your slumber
I – a pilgrim who has not yet found repose
and is woken every morning by the conflagration of the Sun
and an eruption of human faces.
From the heights of your immaculate death
you look down on my confusion…
Do you love me still?
Me, a man who steals at every step
whate'er he desires from other women
and is making a brilliant career
a career without you, Ľudka,
can you still love such a man?

I began working at a hospital. And so began another fairy story.

Primum! nihil nocere!

Once upon a time there was a children's hospital. Over it reigned a queen, who was called The Professor and her right-hand man, The Associate Professor. Every morning, the ladies-in-waiting, maids of honour, domestic staff, footmen and court jesters, all in white, would arrive to pay their respects in the throne room with its view out across the garden.

Her Majesty the Professor acknowledged her underlings with a barely perceptible eye movement, then she took out a stethoscope and carefully checked everyone's heart rate. If satisfied, she would smile and nod. She never spoke. But if she raised an eyebrow, the Associate Professor, standing a little way off, would briskly attach the rubber cap of an electroencephalograph to the subject who had aroused her suspicions and switch on the machine. All you could hear against the background of total silence was the scratchy sound of the recorder. Her Majesty The Professor kept her eyebrow raised until she'd checked through the entire record. Her contented smile would eventually be restored, much to everyone's relief. Another working day could commence.

Then came blood tests. The doctors and nurses lined up with hypodermic syringes held aloft in their hands. At a command from the Associate Professor the various teams dispersed to the wards. Mums would poke the tiny hands of their offspring out through the cots: 'Here you are, go on, do it here.' At the end of the corridor stood the Associate Professor, keeping count of the test tubes of blood. Everyone kept daily, weekly and monthly records of the millilitres planned for and actually turned in. In addition there were columns for the number of X-rays prescribed and the overall dosages of radiation, and the number of urinary catheters, lumbar punctures and punctures of the cerebral ventricles introduced. The record forms ended with the box headed "Medicines".

Cum grano salis

Every first Monday in the month Her Majesty the Professor carried out an appraisal of the work of her subjects. The solemn announcement of the winners began with the ceremony known as Renewing the Associate Professor's Eggs (RAPE). Allegedly it had once been called Checking the Associate Professor's Eggs (CAPE), but, with the passage of time, renewal had become a regular part of the ritual.

The Associate Professor would sit in an armchair in the Hall of Ceremonies, wearing his white coat and with his feet poking out from under it. Her Majesty the Professor would step solemnly up to him and with a quick snap of her shiny teeth she would bite off each of his testicles. She would then turn to us, her subjects, slightly blood-stained about the mouth, and at one go swallow the testicles with sheer sensual pleasure. The Associate Professor pulled on his trousers and then came the ceremony of Checking Subjects' Eggs (CSE). Goodness knows why CSE never became RSE, though that was probably because the subjects, having witnessed CSE, never needed any renewal.

We would approach Her Majesty the Professor's armchair, report form in hand. She would then peruse them while at the same time sticking her hand down a subject's trousers or up her skirt. I didn't know that girls could also have balls, but HM did.

Her hand was ice-cold, but a real turn-on. We longed for her touch in keen anticipation. We hoped she would be satisfied and that after checking our eggs she would also touch our erect member. There was nothing more thrillingly erotic…

Her Majesty the Professor was studying my report form. Suddenly her cold hand stiffened. She raised an eyebrow and glanced up at me, which she'd never done before. Her hand sprang back into life and she subjected my testicles to a thorough palpation. She gave a laugh. Then I felt a squeeze followed at once by pain. Her face went red and her eyes popped out of their sockets as she crushed me.

There and then, in the presence of all the others, she extracted my penis from my trousers and using the blood streaming from it she crossed right through the "Children cured" box that I'd deliberately added to my report.

mea culpa

I had been transferred to the neonatal department to deputise for the consultant, who was away on holiday.

I surveyed the huge incubators with those tiny bodies, their little chests struggling for breath, their flimsy ribs trying to poke through the skin, and their tiny legs, no bigger than an adult finger, scrabbling away like prisoners digging a tunnel to freedom.

The consultant had sole charge of the department so after his departure I was the only doctor there. "You can have no more than three patients die on you in the three weeks I'm away," he set the goalposts for me as he was leaving. Two made their exit the very first night. A baby girl weighing only a kilo packed it in even before the stroke of midnight, having given up the pursuit of oxygen molecules and taken herself off to a place where there are things far more important than oxygen. They brought the little boy to me from surgery at three in the morning. His abdomen had separated and his intestines were held in a little plastic bag. The surgeon explained that they intended to reinsert them gradually into his abdominal cavity, which could be stitched back together in three or four months' time. The little boy took a different view. He told the surgeons and me where to stuff it and died in the early hours of the morning. By six I'd got the paperwork done. Brilliant. I went and lay down.

Shortly thereafter a nurse entered the inspection room. Only the night light was on. She stripped naked and lay down next to me. I found one of her nipples and started drinking hot milk from it. She smeared some healing ointment over her hands and rubbed it into my sore testicles.

Eventually I dropped off.

Amor vincit omnia

Ľudka didn't come and visit me in the department even once. Neither that night, nor any other time. She didn't appear to me, she didn't come in a dream, and she didn't tell me what to do.

What would have happened if she had come? What would have happened if she'd lived, if she'd become – as had been her wish – a paediatrician and we'd worked alongside each other at the children's hospital? Would things have been different?

Certainly.

She would certainly have blocked Her Majesty the Professor's entry to my trousers, she would certainly have cosseted my eggs until they grew to such a size that HM would have choked on them if she tried to bite them off.

Then we'd have ticked off all the boxes together. Wow!

And all those report forms!

And in the evenings we'd have made a pot of tea and leafed through the album containing photos of all the Children Cured and Mums Put at Their Ease and Children Spared Pointless Punctures and X-rays and Children Who Smiled Again and Children Cured Without Superfluous Drugs…

Wow!

But Ľudka never came.

The revolution came instead.

That morning, we were in the throne room as usual. Her Majesty the Professor took up her stethoscope and summoned the first of us to her. This was the colleague who'd been on night duty, Terka. Terka stepped across to HM, undid her coat and let it fall to the ground. HM raised an eyebrow, placed the stethoscope on her exposed breasts and listened for a moment, her eyebrow still raised. Then she made to slip one hand inside Terka's panties. At which point something unprecedented happened. Terka grabbed Her Majesty firmly by the wrist and pushed it away, then she took her panties off. She stood there naked and at ease, with only her nipples aiming at the Professor. The tension lasted only a moment. The Professor was about to raise a hand towards Terka's genitals when another female colleague, Marta, stood up, shed her white coat, bra and panties and just stood there. Her lead was followed at once by Júlia and Jozef and Ondrej and Kristína and

Karol and Elvíra and me and Petra and Fero and Ilona and all the others. Then the Associate Professor did likewise. We stood there naked, dazed by our sudden power. Then we raised our report forms and took them to HM. Terka, Marta, Júlia, Jozef, Ondrej, Kristína, Karol, Elvíra, me, Petra, Fero, Ilona and all the others. We tossed them towards her throne, some onto her lap, the Associate Professor aimed his into her face, and then we just left her to her own devices. We came out into the section where the nurses were waiting with their syringes and needles at the ready. We went from ward to ward and the nurses set down their hypodermics, cast off their uniforms and joined us. The new mums stretched out their babies' little arms and said "Here, do it here," but when they saw us, they too stripped off. We opened all the windows and doors and went outside. It was November and snow had fallen in the night, but no one felt the cold. Hordes of naked people streamed out from every department and the snow beneath our bare feet melted away to nothing and the green patches of grass began to blossom with gaily coloured flowers.

Out through the door of the throne room with its view onto the garden came Her Majesty. No one paid her the slightest bit of notice.

She was naked.

The bell has tolled and the tale is told.

Tam pro toto

The papers started saying that Ľudka's killers were innocent.

The department's stocks of saline started to get low.

The hospital's management decided that we should choose a new Professor.

They were alleged to be victims of the communist regime.

Some said I should apply.

I discovered that our little patient Samko might have the genetic disease that had just been described in the *Journal of Pediatrics*.

Petra suggested that perhaps I ought not to apply, given that I'd held office under the old regime.

The attorney general decided that they should be released from prison.

Antibiotics fell into short supply.

Samko's condition could be verified by genetic screening in Paris.

In a secret ballot my colleagues elected me to run the hospital.

Petra applied for the job of Professor.

The trial, it was said, should be re-run, because certain mistakes had occurred.

I sent a blood sample to Paris.

Petra came in one day with a suitcase full of antibiotics, a gift from the makers, she said.

I wrote a letter to *Pravda* insisting that the murder of a nineteen-year-old girl is not a blow directed against Communism.

The screening carried out in Paris confirmed that Samko was suffering from the genetic disease described in the *Journal of Pediatrics*.

Petra came out on top and became the new Professor.

I received no response from *Pravda*.

Petra went off to a conference in Brasil. On her return, report forms were reinstated.

Samko died. Petra said we should have treated him with the new drug we'd had donated.

There was still no sign of Ľudka.

The new forms had but one section – "Drugs".

Petra did not re-introduce either RAPE or CAPE; Petra oversaw the issue of medicines.

The *Journal of Pediatrics* published a piece on the successful treatment of Samko's disorder by transplanting stem cells.

Petra went off to a conference in Japan.

Mums stuck the arms of their babies out and cried: "Give us the drugs, here, do it here…"

The country was divided into two parts.

Samko had two siblings, and a screening carried out in Paris confirmed that both had the same genetic disease as Samko. They suggested a transplant.

No one knew who should re-run the murder trial, so it wasn't re-run at all.

I tried to insist that the importing and stocking of drugs should fall within the remit of the hospital management.

On her return from a conference in Honolulu, Petra insisted that Samko's siblings be given a new, untried drug. I refused.

Ľudka's murderers were issued with passports and some of them set up in business.

Stem cell transplants as carried out in Paris, though still only experimentally, was our only hope, but mortality continued to run at over fifty per cent. Tests had shown that any other treatments were ineffectual and only aggravated the condition.

Drug supply was controlled by the new board of directors

appointed by the health minister.

I applied to the Ministry for permission to have my patients treated abroad.

Petra was at a conference in Mexico.

I refused to fill in the new report forms.

Samko's siblings died.

The hospital's elected management team was discharged.

Petra phoned from Sydney to charge me with neglecting to treat Samko and his siblings and refusing to keep records of my work.

In both regards she was right.

Ibis redibis Nunquam peribis

Clearly, I couldn't remain at the children's hospital. I had failed as a doctor, I had failed as a manager. I had failed as a human being.

On the morning of my departure, a rep from that company came asking to see me.

"My name is Horst," he introduced himself, "Good morning, doctor, have you got a minute?"

I led him to my office and made him a coffee. You'll get nowhere with me anyway, I mused.

"Oh, thank you! I just want to show you something."

He laid his attaché case on my desk, opened it and took from it something like a laptop. It was The Instrument.

"You were among the first to diagnose that rare genetic disease. As you will recall, you had to send a DNA sample to Paris. Well now, doctor, you needn't any more. Look!"

From his bag he took a little bottle containing a small amount of a red liquid.

"This is a sample of a patient's blood."

Through the dropper on the end of the bottle he expelled a tiny drop of blood into a minuscule opening in The Instrument. The display started to flicker, different coloured dots joined up into lines that twisted and danced, merged, formed patterns that shaded into each other, intermingled, and then re-emerged like some living primeval matter until the computer stopped whirring and a final image appeared on the screen. Then Horst pressed a key on the keyboard and the image changed into a system of curved lines, graphs and numbers. He clicked again, the bright dots began to run together and on the screen you could see the clear outlines of an embryo that kept changing as in a speeded-up film. Before our very eyes the typical structures of branchial arches came and went, the organs – heart, lungs – were created and the brain and spinal chord grew out of the neural plate; the head took shape, with eyes and a face that grew clearer and clearer, then suddenly the image changed and we had before us a complete newborn, which went on developing into a toddler and, lo and behold! – I recognised the face, yes, it was he, Samko...

Horst clicked again and the image grew still.

"Did you recognise your patient, doctor?"

He showed at the age when I first saw him in our department. The age when he'd begun to be tormented by fevers, rashes, lassitude and total exhaustion.

I nodded. Horst restarted the display. It didn't take long. Samko grew thin, shrinking away until his tormented features became composed in the very last image.

"Now, Doctor, look at this."

He clicked back to the previous display with the graphs and figures.

He pointed to one sequence that was highlighted in red. I recognised the pattern of Samko's genetic defect.

Horst invited me to a training course. I couldn't refuse.

Alex intervent

It was my very last night duty. I roamed the corridors and felt alienated.

I had always seen my future linked to this place. I'd imagined spending the productive years of my life here. From the cots of my tiny patients I would repel all viruses, bacteria, autoimmune and oncogenous clones, here I'd protect them from solar eruptions, geological anomalies, meteorites, I'd treat the injuries done them by evil parents, crazy teachers, mad drivers, slimy paedophiles, alcohol, tobacco and drugs, friends with little heads and big muscles. Here I desired to fill in the "Children cured" rubric. Instead of which a quite different one was proliferating day by day.

"Every doctor has his own graveyard," Professor Hruška, our pathology lecturer used to say. "He alone knows how many of its denizens he couldn't have helped, and how many he actually helped get there."

I recalled my first night duty in the neonatal department. I'd gone onto the ward. I saw the little lights on the instruments twinkling into the half-light, the displays on the monitors tracing curves, and the little white bodies in incubators shining like angels with broken wings, trapped in cages and attached to the cots with tubes and probes.

Also on duty that night was the nurse who'd treated my damaged testicles that first night. She was feeding a tiny patient from a bottle that she was holding through the incubator window. A latter-day Madonna and Child, it occurred to me.

"I've come to say good-bye," I said.

"You're leaving... That's a real shame." She gently finished feeding and offered me her hand: "Good luck!"

I put my arms round her; she didn't resist. Through her freshly starched uniform I could feel not the breasts that had saved my life that morning, but the scratchy embroidered logo of a pharmaceutical company that she had on her blouse.

I undid a button on her chest, meaning to let my hand bid farewell to her nipples, to drink one last time of that warm, life-giving milk.

No go. The logo was stitched through to her skin.

Gaudeamus igitur

We celebrated our school-leaving exams in the Municipal Tavern, right next to the school. We'd used to go there even before then, albeit in fear of running into one or other of our teachers… Now we were grown-ups!

My classmates and I had several beers each, chasing them down with garlic toast and when we mounted the steep steps to leave it was already evening. The fresh air and warm outdoors set my head spinning. For one last time we went up to the school gates, which were locked, singing our hearts out. The world was a great place for living.

We'd come through, we'd made good!

The windows we'd spent four years of our life behind were in darkness.

Actually no – a film was being projected on them, accelerated black-and-white images.

Ai, zde leží zem ta, před okem mým slzy ronícím
někdy kolébka, nyní národa mého rakev…

The total current entering a junction must equal the total current leaving the junction; the sum of the squares on the hypotenuse is equal to the sum of the squares on the other two sides; a body immersed in a fluid…

Ω ΞΕΙΝ, ΑΓΓΕΛΛΕΙΝ ΛΑΚΕΔΑΙΜΟΝΙΟΙΣ ΟΤΙ ΤΗΔΕ ΚΕΙΜΕΘΑ, ΤΟΙΣ ΚΕΙΝΩΝ ΡΗΜΑΣΙ ΠΕΙΘΟΜΕΝΟΙ.

Прогласъ ѥсмь свѧтоу єваньгелию:
Яко пророци прорекли сѫтъ прѣждє,
Христъ грѧдетъ събьратъ ѩзыкъ,
Свѣтъ бо єстъ вьсемоу мироу семоу.

Ceterum censeo Carthaginem esse delendam!

Я к вам пишу — чего же боле?
Что я могу еще сказать?
Теперь, я знаю, в вашей воле
Меня презреньем наказать.

Liberté, égalité, fraternité!

Sur le pont d'Avignon…

London's burning, London's burning.
Fetch the engines, fetch the engines.
Fire fire…

Freude, schöner Götterfunken,
Tochter aus Elysium,
wir betreten feuertrunken,
himmlische, dein Heiligtum

Cogito, ergo sum!

Marína moja! teda tak sme my
ako tie božie plamene,
ako tie kvety v chladnej zemi,
ako tie drahé kamene;
padajú hviezdy, aj my padneme,
vädnú tie kvety, aj my zvädneme,
a klenoty hruda kryje:
Ale tie hviezdy predsa svietili,
a pekný život tie kvety žili,
a diamant v hrude nezhnije!

Gaudeamus igitur
Iuvenes dum sumus.
Post iucundam iuventutem
Post molestam senectutem
Nos habebit humus.

That first cigarette.   *A mantes*
                                               sunt amentes

That timid embrace on the ski tow, "so you don't fall off the T-bar".

Playing footsie under the desk.

Oh my God, what begins at the point where the miniskirt ends?

Whispering.

Copying from one's neighbour.

Sending notes.

Seeing her off.

Hands! Oh those kind, delicate, tiny hands!

Her head nestling on one's shoulder.

Hugs.

That first kiss.

Kisses, kisses, kisses…

The whispers, the ecstasy of touching, annoying zips, muddy dresses, the last buses missed, the transparent excuses.

But actual love-making, no, no, not yet.

Let's do it today. The ultimate, the forbidden, the dangerous, the sweetest thing of all.

We did it.

We were grown-ups.

Memento mori

From Košice to Bratislava it's about four hundred kilometres. Eight hours by train. Nine crowns a minute on the phone.

We were learning embryology. Ľudka from Comenius, I from Šafárik.

People decide about the life or death of an unborn child the first time its heart gives a beat. In the fifth week there's the first electrical signal in the special cells of the myocard and the muscle contracts for the first time. Boom. After that it just goes on, non-stop, without a break, tirelessly, to the very end of life. Boom-boom. Boom-boom. The heart, that seat of life, that symbol of love. Independent of the brain, working unerringly away at its own pace according to the needs of the body. It's its own boss, it's self-driven, self-nourishing, self-oxygenating. It needs no one. It's got plenty of common sense. If the brain starts interfering in its job, life is put at risk.

Our little angel arrived to save us. He did the best he could. He snuggled down in a cosy spot in the womb and set about the miracle task whereby something arises out of nothing. He settled like a sad butterfly on our foreheads and in his quiet little butterfly voice spoke to us: "Never fear, we can do it, we can definitely do it. Who else if not us?

We didn't listen.

He was outshouted by other voices.

What?
Now?
Where?
Exams!
Somewhere to live?
Study!
Live!
What on?

And other voices:

Nappies.
Ailments.
Crèche.
Sleep.

And those mantras … :

Responsibility.
Talent.
Gratitude.
Ingratitude.
Disappointment.
Trust.
Hope.
Investment.
Shame.

The butterfly fluttered its wings and screamed: We can do it! We can do it!

The tiny heart grew and beat ever louder. Boom-boom! Boom-boom! Ready to fight on, fight on our behalf and for our benefit until we died. And even longer.

We met all the conditions, the termination board gave its consent.

It was inevitable.

Nobody was listening to our frightened little butterfly.

When you kill a carp at Christmas you see its heart beating long after you remove it from its dead host. It is independent. It needs no one. It gets on with its job even though there's no more point.

But it does stop eventually.

The heart of our little angel who had come to save us beat for two weeks.

| REQUIEM |

I attended the funeral in my school graduation suit, which I'd also worn to my exams. I bought a new white shirt and a black tie.

There's a spot on Košice station where I saw her for the last time. A month before, I had hugged her and waved after the departing train until her head in the window disappeared round the first bend. I used to be superstitious. I would always keep waving till the last moment. I was afraid I might not see her again.

It was sad that she was leaving, but she radiated an inner happiness. She kept smiling. Her eyes shone with all the touches, all the kisses that I'd managed to shower her with between Friday and Sunday. There'd been the trip to the cottage, the visit to see Julo, dinner at the Carpano, football on TV and Panenka's perfect eleven, Karol Polák's "We're the champions of Europe!" and the late, warm spring that left green stains of the young grass on my trousers. Our last lovemaking under a tree in the park after midnight...

We talked of having sixteen children. Ideally all at once. Sedecimuplets.

Or was it not like that? Could her look from the window of the departing train have no longer been for me? Was she going back to the city where she'd spent the last year, where her first exhilarating exams – biology and histology – lay ahead of her? Was she keen to get back to her hall of residence that throbbed with the student life of a metropolis?

Or were her eyes gazing even farther afield, far, far, faraway...? Was it *joy*, or something else? Was it more than a farewell for four weeks, more than a memory of the last three days? Was our whole life together, nearly a thousand days of it, running through her mind?

Now I was travelling in the same direction as she back then. The train had passed Ružín, the lake in which we'd clumsily tried to have sex under water, it had passed the Slovak Paradise, where we'd camped in a forbidden spot and got up to other forbidden things, and the Tatras, where we drank of the limpid waters of the River Belá and went skinny-dipping like they did in *Copper Tower*, that film of 1970. We whooshed past the shieling at Štrba, where it had all begun, with me feeling her mohair jumper under her anorak while we were on a potato-picking stint. The train stopped at Žilina for quite a while. That was where she'd come with me to a league game. We also stopped at Trenčín, where we'd recently been to the 'City of Fashion' exhibition. Then the gloomy, so very gloomy station at Piešťany, the place where we said our farewells after I'd been to visit her...

At the Pathology Department in Bratislava the door was opened by an orderly. His eyes softened when I introduced myself and explained why I was there. A moment later he was back with a small package and his index finger placed on his lips.

Histology slides.

I'll never let on to anyone. But a bit of Ľudka will always be with me. And who's to say: one day it might be possible to reconstruct her in her entirety… Yes, I'm sure it will. I just wonder if she'll remember me. Hm… I may have to explain everything to her… about belonging to me, about having always belonged to me…

I bought a huge bunch of white carnations. I clasped it to my bosom like the baby that was never born to us. I went to the crematorium, which was already packed, though I saw no one.

The body that I had so loved lay a few yards in front of me. The wooden coffin on the bier was closed, but I had an acute physical sense of her proximity. I leaned forward so as to be as close as possible. I was dying to go up to the coffin, cast aside the cover and touch her. To kiss her one last time, stroke her hands, hair… The white carnations on the lid were alive, and she too was alive. Just a moment longer…

Just a moment longer and that wondrous creation of Nature will be swallowed up by the crematory furnace and turned into a handful of ash.

And her soul? Where is Ľudka's soul? Is she looking down on me from somewhere? I'm left alone, my love, all alone…

The Dean's address, police cameras, music.

As the coffin began to slide downwards, I wanted to stand up and hurl myself after her. No matter where, but where you go, I go too, my love. They'll not keep us apart, ever!

Absently I accepted people's condolences. I heard someone say:

"I'm sorry, but the corpse was in a terrible state, in this heat decomposition had progressed very rapidly. The skin on her head had peeled away, so she had no hair, and her face was disfigured beyond recognition. And the stench was so extreme that she couldn't be left in the coffin. During the service the only thing inside the coffin was the urn with her ashes. We had to cremate her yesterday."

I went outside. The urn grove was more like a parched steppe. I was alone on the scorched earth, there was no atmosphere, no oxygen, no ozone, just the blazing sun and little me, unprotected from the cosmic radiation.

৵

I stopped reading; it was far into the night.

I came down into the living room to put a log on the smouldering embers. The tall candles stood guard, immobile, over the darkness. I went outside.

During the day, the peace and quiet of the back garden was not disturbed by the traffic in the street, and at night not even the light from the street lamps reached that far. I sat briefly on the cold bench; it was from there that we had often done a spot of stargazing, particularly in August when we used to watch Perseid meteors falling.

Ha, flashes of eternity...

"Anything we see happening overhead with the stars actually happened hundreds and thousands of years ago," he taught me. "I wonder what's going on there now, at this very moment... And which is the more true? The reality we're witnessing that hasn't existed for years, or the reality of which we know nothing beyond the fact that it is?"

That Colleague of my husband's, the one he treated for depression after he attempted suicide... Odd.

I knew about the murdered student girl, everybody did. My husband and I never spoke of it. He often mentioned his Colleague, but never the girl, and I do wonder why. When all's said and done it was only one murder among many; I never understood why this one was so exceptional.

But why did he never mention it?

Wait though, yes, now I remember. He did once. That Colleague had a great love that was taken away from him, he said, but that was all. But then everyone has lost at least one love, so what of it?

"He was a weakling," he would say of him. "And the weak should be helped. Even if they're bastards."

Odd, that.

But is there anything odd about an oddball being a bit odd? If an oddball weren't odd, that would be odd!

I felt cold.

I went back to the bedroom and read on.

But not out loud now.

Never again.

Nunquam.

NOTEBOOK № 2

Aut viam inveniam
aut faciam!

Horst's DNA-testing Instrument sold like hot cakes.

First I went to see my pals in the big hospitals and they all wanted one. The only problem was money.

Ružena from Martin organised a collection, in support of which I lent her some photos of Samko and his siblings. Karol became Deputy Director at Košice and insisted they got one. Patrícia in Nitra held a colloquium to which she invited their Director. At the informal get-together after the lectures we gave the Director a demonstration using his own blood. What The Instrument didn't show was his blood-alcohol level. Žilina bought a more advanced version to get one over on Martin. In Bratislava, the example of the Ladislav Dérer Hospital at Kramáre was followed by the Mickiewicz and Ružinov hospitals and St Michael's

Military Hospital. Prešov was a hard nut to crack. But we invited the Director to a colloquium in San Francisco, where I acted as his personal tour guide for a week. He bought ten. Each Instrument was supplied with enough microchips for fifty tests. So sales of chips took off. I launched a special bulletin for our customers. I arranged seminars in Trnava, Trenčín, Banská Bystrica, Liptovský Mikuláš, Poprad, Michalovce, Humenné, Majorca and Bali. My lecturers included Ružena, Karol and Patrícia, who had the largest patient databases. I set up a limited company and took on a secretary and bookkeeper. I got to know personally all the Directors of all the hospitals and research institutes in Slovakia. And on first-name terms. I had to open a branch in Prague. Then others in Warsaw and Budapest. I became top salesman in Central and Eastern Europe. Those of us involved with The Instrument became one big, close-knit family.

I blessed the day when Petra got the job. She had to listen to what companies had to say. And I was a company. She enjoyed every invitation to dinner; I was the one who did the inviting. She lived in hope of receiving a fee for her lectures; I was the one who decided who would receive a fee and how much. She minced words; I could be quite blunt. She had to hide from both her superiors and her minions; I just got on with my job and everybody was happy.

I signed up for a pilot's course and parachute lessons and bought a small plane. I started playing golf. At one tournament I ran into Černý. The little Young Commnist with the big prick who, that time in the sauna, said he'd have me demoted to Pioneer. He'd put on a bit of weight and his black mega-moustache and bushy beard now covered the entire lower half of his face. He'd got rich and knew everybody worth knowing. He greeted me with a broad smile and firm handshake like any of those men who are masters of their own destiny and the destinies of those who cross their paths. All the indications were that he'd quite forgotten the incident in the sauna. We were playing together and at the ninth hole he suggested a strategy of 'DNA analysis at every GP surgery'. At the twelfth it was a state subsidy. And at the eighteenth a subsidy for him.

The people of Slovakia became the best genetically mapped population in the world. *The thing is that we shouldn't ever have to be ashamed of anything we've done, Doc…*

Per vias naturales   *Veni vidi vici*

Well then, I should have been quite content. For my business it had been a highly successful day.

It hadn't got off to a good start. I'd slept badly, and I woke up badly. My innards were having a tough time coping with the residues of the previous night's dinner with Peter Spružina, Director of the University Hospital.

For as long as I can remember, I've had trouble emptying my bowels properly.

Urinating was different. There you can see what's what. You can talk to it, coax it: "Come on now, what are you waiting for? There, there…," or put a bit more menace into it: "Get on with it! How long do we have to hang around here? I'm fed up of this lark, stupid! Did we come here for a pee or just to gawp at each other?" And eventually it'll give in, sooner or later it'll do what's asked of it, relax the sphincter muscles and stop messing you about.

But round the back you can't see anything. You can't talk to it. There's not even anything there to talk to. You can scarcely produce a thing, or, if you're in luck, a minor explosion will shake the world, though you don't know what'll come next. Is that all I wanted to tell the world today?

No matter how long I sat there, there was always something left inside. I would always stand up with a sense of a job not quite done. The space inside that had become available was like an open wound, like flesh with the skin torn away. The walls that had been tense suddenly grew limp, gasping briefly for breath and looking round in disbelief until they calmed down. But lurking in a corner somewhere there was still an unsolved problem that thrust itself more and more into the centre ground. Its immediate environment having become deflated, its own unfulfilled, or rather unevacuated, ambitions came to the fore, surfacing with a kind of quiet insistence. I would often have to face a dilemma: had the situation been resolved sufficiently for me to go on my way, or was it better not to chance it, even if it made me late? It sometimes happened that the problem of the unfinished task manifested itself at some point between start and finish of my morning journey to work, and a number of comically embarrassing episodes fell short of a happy ending. Sometimes it was a matter of seconds and the excruciating ride in the lift might not have ended without mishap. Critical instants could be affected by apparently trifling considerations. Unfortunately, the residue might not have the consistency of the morning's output and the sphincters might not be up to their task. The morning chitchat in the lift, which could be about politics, sport or just the weather, were a serious test of my acting skills and yoga-inspired self-control.

Victory – if ever it transpired – was a perfect triumph of the spirit over the dark forces of nature, and the relief and sheer delight went to the top of the table of the *joys* that man's existence may bring him. *Ad Libitum*

Spružina thought we might go up to the television tower on Kamzík Hill for dinner.

We reminisced about our time in the Socialist Youth Union and didn't let business matters spoil our meal. Looking out from the rotating restaurant, we took in the outlines of Bratislava by night – proud metropolis of a young country filled with ambition.

"Our dealings, my friend, are based on the friendly terms I enjoy with the Minister. And on our own precious friendship. It's up to you to show how much you appreciate it."

I was no greenhorn and I knew how much fertiliser such relationships required in order to flourish. In order for my precious friend to continue banging on about 'friendship'.

For starters we had a delicate carpaccio of sirloin, cream of broccoli soup and toasted baguette. To follow we had baked catfish with apple chutney and potato wedges. For dessert pancakes flambé with chocolate and whipped cream. We had Bošáca plum brandy as an aperitif, Mrva Stanko white ruland to go with the catfish – two bottles sufficed – and six-puttonyos Tokaj with the pancakes.

He declined to take a cab back and summoned his chauffeur. The University Hospital couldn't afford a new car, so he was using the old Tatra 613.

"Why waste money on a taxi, my friend, my pal Paulie here will drive us. We can't come from work in a taxi, can we now? What would people think? And let me teach you something, my friend – and this is important, so remember: When you're eating, keep your mouth closed and don't slurp!" *Historia magistra vitae*

"Don't smoke in here," Elena whispered, carefully closing the bedroom door. "The kid sleeps in the next room." She poured me a cognac in a thick-bottomed glass and put a record on low on the old gramophone.

She lived in a tower block not far from the city centre. I'd asked Paulie to let me off there. I was feeling nostalgic for the old days. Elena, the culture rep with a perfect body who I had liberated from the sauna...

"Have fun, my friend," said Spružina as we parted. "And tomorrow don't be late. I'm expecting you at seven-thirty, we've got papers to sign. I'll show you how it all works; you'll be surprised. The money'll be in your account from the off, so you can do all the necessary." He thought a moment, as if staring into the far distance, then he declared: "Genetics, it'll be all go from now on."

"How's business?" Elena enquired.

"Good, excellent... Today I bought the Health Minister," I said, settling down on the sofa and propping my feet next to my empty glass on the little coffee table. "Tomorrow I'll have the Prime Minister as well."

"He won't cost you much though, will he?"

"We pair at golf. The tournament at Černý's."

She jumped at the name. In spite of herself her eyes flashed towards the nursery door. Hell, I'd forgotten how helpless she'd looked that time on our training course and what had followed. So many years had passed. She quickly regained control.

"What? The Prime Minister in a golf tournament at Černý's? Both cocks of our very own dunghill? I like that! One of them won't survive though," she added, forcing a smile. She poured me another glass.

"Never mind, it's all working a treat. Tomorrow I'll tell him: Congratulations, Prime Minister, the system you've created couldn't be better." I was beginning to slur my words slightly. "The objectives are clear, the costs are clear, no one need play games, no one need have any bloody qualms. Dinner's served. Cornucopia. All you need do is turn up, sit down and help yourself. Sometimes not even that: the food'll leap into your mouth of its own accord."

I glanced at her. Poured myself a cognac and took a sip. "That bathrobe suits you."

"You woke us up. We'd already gone to bed."

"You still got no one?"

"No, I've got Irma," she said, again with that sad smile.

"She must be quite big now…"

"Yes, quite the little lady… It's been a long time…"

"And… you're okay?"

"You know how it is, journalism these days isn't a job with the cheapest insurance premiums. You never know what direction you'll get it in the neck from. On the other hand… It's certainly interesting, probably more interesting than anything else. We hoped that in gratitude for the freedom we'd been given we'd all want to be kind and just. But so far, that's not how it's looking. Freedom has stirred the worst in us. A just society hasn't been born yet. For now, the birth canals are just oozing blood and mucus with an admixture of faeces and urine from the adjacent orifices. As they said in ancient Rome: *Inter urinas et faeces nascimur*... It's great to be on hand though. Observing and writing things down."

Ensconced as I was, I began to feel tired, my eyes starting to flicker. I yawned.

"Mmm..., I don't think much of your taste – mucus, blood, faeces, urine... Lots of kids are born these days by caesarean, all clean and sterile. They don't meet turds till much later, after they've grown a bit..." I said, trying to make light of it.

"Justice has to fight its own corner. History hasn't so far known a surgeon who would ease a new order into the world by caesarean section. True, some would-be virtuosi have had a go, but either the baby proved not viable, or the mother died in childbirth, or usually both."

"So when may we expect the infant of universal justice?"

"Quite soon. I'm thinking of writing an article about you tomorrow. About how a good doctor and talented poet turned into a bloodsucking parasite. History is always made up of the stories of individuals. You do realise that with your business dealings you're writing history, don't you? That all those tables creaking under your cornucopia are a pointer to your own downfall? That the food that flies into your mouth doesn't come from Heaven, but from the tables of other people?"

"Are you still a communist?"

"This isn't a matter of ideology. It's as plain as the nose on your face, though admittedly, it's getting ever harder to tell good from evil. We used to joke that anyone who didn't steal was robbing his family. We don't make jokes like that any more. An A+ in thievery is the basic requirement for the successful businessman or politician. It won't be long before we start consigning freaks who pay their taxes and never exceed the speed limit to the asylum. But the more a narrow circle of people takes, the greater will be the pain that follows. The mother of the new order of justice will suffer more, but the birth will be quicker. And more blood may flow in the process. You'll see! And your type will be the first to cop it."

Her sleepy eyes were getting back the spark of militancy that I knew of yore, and with the abrupt movements of her head her hair undulated like the sea. I stood up and clasped her recalcitrant head in my hands.

"Don't you think you're exaggerating a bit? These days nobody goes hungry. People have never had it so good."

"True. We eat so much that we never feel hungry, we have so much sex that we never long for it and we work so hard that work affords us no pleasure any more."

"You have so much sex that … ?"

"Do you remember how we used to dream of a world of justice?" she said, pretending not to hear. "Do you remember asking, way back, that Young Communist League functionary woman if some of us might not come to believe that luxury was ours by right, something that we deserved because of our status and importance? Do you remember how we later read Mayakovskii together? How we wanted to give popular taste a slap in the face? And how we played Plato's *Socrates' Defence*?" she said, her voice softer now as she looked me straight in the eye.

"Yes. The panel on the 'ideologically engaged literature' competition disqualified us on the grounds that Plato's philosophy was idealist..."

"So then we used Sládkovič's translation of Voltaire and it all went fine."

"And nobody minded that Sládkovič was a priest..."

"Well, we did tinker with it a bit..." We both laughed.

I got the urge to kiss her.

"I need a fag," I said.

"Come out on the balcony."

Even in the city, the night air is full of summer memories.

We stood by the rail. I blew thick puffs of smoke as the music played quietly behind us.

I put my arm around her, the cigarette still between my fingers.

"I used to want to go to the Caucasus and live like Khlebnikov. Wandering about the mountains, writing poetry, creating a language of my own..."

For a brief while we danced. She put her arms round my neck and allowed me to hold her closer. I could feel the softness of her breasts against my chest.

"I'm dancing with the most beautiful culture rep in Slovakia," I whispered in her ear.

"That was the most wonderful time of my life," she said. "We were strong and we were right. No stupid committee could take that from us."

"And this, O men of Athens, is the truth and the whole truth; I have concealed nothing, I have dissembled nothing. And yet I know that this plain speaking makes them hate me, and what is their hatred but evidence that I am speaking the truth? – this is the occasion and reason for their slandering me, as you will discover in this or any future enquiry."

"There you are mistaken: a man who is good for anything ought not to calculate the chances of living or dying; he ought only to consider whether in whatsoever he is doing he is doing right or wrong – acting the part of a good man or bad. […] Let me die next […] and be avenged of my enemy, rather than abide here by the beaked ships, a scorn and a burden of the earth."

"One former good doctor, presently a Bloodsucker and Burden of the Earth, desires to clamp his lips to your jugular veins … ," I said, taking a deep breath. The skin on the nape of her neck was just as delicate as back then.

"When did you last write a poem?" she asked in a whisper.

I don't know whether to blame the cognac or her perfume, but I now asked something I'd never dared ask before:

"Why did you actually keep the baby?"

The skin on her neck crinkled and she pulled away.

"I could have come off even worse, you realise; like if I'd married you," she said, running her fingers across her brow and giving a terse laugh. The record ended, she set it aside and turned the gramophone off.

"When did you last write a poem?" she repeated the question

into the sudden silence. I don't know whether her steady gaze meant to convey more disappointment or disdain.

"I don't know, a long time ago, I forget. I don't want to think about it. It might have been the one… the one for you…

I sense you are on tenterhooks
when to talk to me you deign.
No, you mustn't be, fear me not,
no, I shan't fail you again."

"Do you know what's dawned on me? We're all either robots or people. The robots among us are programmed to do their best to ensure that they function. People do everything to ensure that how they function makes sense. And it's getting harder and harder to find a real person among the robots…"

A sleepy voice called from the nursery: "Muuum!"

She sighed.

"The night is a bank from which to borrow time. We pay off the debt as soon as we can, and the interest at the end of our days."

These aphorisms of hers were getting a bit much for me. I wonder if she was right about that surfeit of sex.

"You must go now," she said.

I was quite ready for bed anyway. I had to see Spružina at half past seven.

Papers to sign. *Omnia causa fiunt*

The first cornucopia I ever found was when I was eight. On the last day of the summer holidays a consignment of teaching aids had been unloaded in the school playground. The caretaker probably wasn't in, so there was this unguarded pile of textbooks, exercise books, rulers, pencils and pens. All I had to do was scramble over the fence and help myself. Then it was off home with my booty, making sure nobody saw me, and into some secret hiding-place with it. It was a wonderful feeling, to be in possession of stolen goods. Something that was mine that I hadn't had to buy, spend money on. Sometimes I would sit and gaze on my lovely pile of brand new exercise books. Copybooks with wide lines for first years, blank blue ones, others lined gloriously in red, yet others squared in green, ideal for playing battleships or noughts and crosses.

An exercise book is for writing or drawing things in and then showing them to someone else. These had never been seen by anyone. I never played battleships or noughts and crosses with anyone. I was afraid that anyone could tell at once that I'd stolen them. Everything I wrote or drew in them was as if lost in a black hole.

I was never found out. The caretaker didn't spot anything missing, no one else asked about anything that was missing, no one carried out an investigation. I slunk about school like a fox, alone in the knowledge of the treasure I had at home and how I had come by it. The sense of superiority over my classmates, who only had a handful of officially issued exercise books, warmed me inside like freshly made grog.

It was like a drug, an endless source of delight: an undiscovered crime, and unpunished.

Radix Omnium Malorum !

The signing of the papers passed off smoothly. Spružina was at his most official. He kept me waiting for about a quarter of an hour: "Klára dear, look after our guest, will you?"

"Have you got a hard day ahead of you?" she asked – one of those questions they get taught at secretarial college.

Something about the way she moved got to me. You know the kind of thing – something that defies definition. It might be the way they lean forward as they set your coffee down on the table, the way they cross their legs as they stand before you, it might be a hand gesture, the expression in their eyes … It's over in no time, but it causes a shift in the tectonic layers that grabs you by the balls and gives your heart such a shot of adrenaline that it accelerates from zero to a hundred in half a second.

"Every day's a hard day, or as hard as you make it," I replied. I couldn't tear my eyes away from her. It was the way her thighs moved. As if beneath her dress she had a light source, a light-house that flashed every now and then to enable ships to find the right way.

"And you, Klára?"

She knew what spot I was looking at. It was nothing deliberate on her part. The lighthouse was a natural component of her being. She couldn't have switched it off even if she'd wanted to. I didn't know yet whether she would want to.

"What about me?"

"Are you also in for a tough day?"

"It's not up to me to decide about my days." It was a witty

come-back, but – complaint or challenge?

"Who does decide about your days then?"

"Work, my studies, my husband…"

Married, then… I'd learned that a husband needn't complicate matters; often quite the reverse. Added to which the existence of one adds a certain piquancy to any victory.

"You're at college?" I asked.

"Alongside my job. Obviously, I wouldn't want to remain a secretary all my life…" Her eyes were translucent and innocent. I wanted her. Right then.

The door leading to the Director's office opened and Spružina entered the room.

"So, my friend, come on in!"

"Klára's been taking good care of me, thank you for the coffee. By the way, she tells me that it's you who decides about her work. I'm off for a game of golf this afternoon, you know, with the Prime Minister, but I don't have a partner yet… Could you perhaps…?"

"You'd like to have young Klára? Well I suppose… why not? Klára, have you ever played golf?"

He didn't wait for her reply.

"Carry on here till ten, do what's needed, then you can pop home and get ready. That's settled, sorted."

Klára seemed to flush, but before she could respond we were inside the Director's office.

"Look at this, my friend… This is what modern management looks like." He pointed with pride at a huge panel fixed to the wall, like a little boy showing off his model railway or stamp collection to his friends.

It was a huge electronic diagram of the hospital. It was like a gigantic gaming machine with numbers flashing on the screen, masses of numbers, each one representing this or that ward or department. The numbers kept changing, flickering, joining up into lines that then merged into great streams or rivers of yellow or gold. The gold rivers had branches, forming a network, while some backwaters ended in little lakes flanked by columns illuminated by numbers that kept going up and up. Some numbers weren't yellow, but red or green, but they didn't change so rapidly.

The Director sat down at the control desk and keyed something in. A new stream and a new column appeared on the screen, a new lake into which little golden streams began to trickle, the numbers shooting up in the lake.

"Now," said Spružina, "I'm going to send you a small advance, but come here, you have to authorise its immediate transfer back." With a broad sweep of his hand he pressed enter. "Right…"

Two new lakes formed and a little gold stream decanted itself by turns into the second, then into the third. But it didn't hang around there for long either, but flowed finally into a mighty river that was garnering in tributaries from all the littler streams. It was like the Amazon basin. Or the circulatory system of the human body. The numbers in the Amazon, the main artery, were rising fastest. *Quod me nutrit me destruit*

All those flashing lights hurt my eyes and the catfish of the day before made itself felt, flicking its tail somewhere inside my belly. I was glad when we were done. Spružina was visibly content.

"What d'you think of it, my friend, fabulous, isn't it? You

don't have to worry about a thing, all the accounting is just as it should be. Invoices, transfers, everything's gets done and dusted automatically. You can go off and play golf now, my old mucker."

At that moment I remembered Elena. I'd just been writing history. Starring Dr Slobberyenot and Dr Bloodsucker. I felt as if the catfish's tail was slapping at my face. All those flashing numbers and gold veins – they were the elaborately distilled and sterilised sighs and cries of the patients within the walls of all the pavilions throughout the hospital complex. The entire machine did one single thing: it converted the red colour of blood and pain into the yellow colour of gold. Though it wasn't actually the machine doing it: the machine merely replicated schematically the actions of people, of Spružina, of me.

The machine was really just a modern version of Her Majesty the Professor's report forms.

You're like Her Majesty, the realisation hit me hard. You're worse than she was. You don't grab people by the balls, you don't look anyone in the eye, you don't see *Their* blood, you don't see *Them*. You just wallow in your heated golden pond and watch as the numbers on the display go up and up.

I felt sick. The catfish in my belly just wouldn't let up.

Your stomach's too small for big fish, I thought.

I was rescued by a broken hospital toilet. Of course there was no paper in it. I tore the freshly signed contract between me and the University Hospital into four pieces, the blood of my and Spružina's signatures not yet properly dry. The stiff paper was scratchy and it wouldn't flush. Time after time the details of our agreement, numbers, totals, names, came floating to the surface.

I hadn't the patience to wait for the cistern to refill, panicking, I flushed with not enough water and again everything came floating back up. I tried desperately to poke the paper into the deepest entrails of the bowl with the lavatory brush, but only for brown-flecked shreds of paper to get tangled in the bristles. In one corner I found a bucket, which I filled at the wash basin and poured into the bowl. At last everything disappeared round the S-bend. Exhausted, I went out into the corridor and fled from the management building. I made my way at speed between the pavilions, heading for the way out.

At the windows of the wards *They* stood. Sick people in dressing gowns, pale-faced, silent and staring after me.

With a squeaking sound they part-opened those old, peeling windows, spread the black wings of their dressing gowns and swarmed together in a silent throng above my head. I could sense their cold, bad breath on the nape of my neck, I wanted to run, but was suddenly powerless, all the bones in my body began to rattle, my sight misted over and all I could see was the absent stares in their eyes, projecting from their cadaverous skulls.

They saw me off the premises. I was cold; with shaking, ice-cold fingers I unlocked my BMW and hastily turned the ignition.

The main thing is that all the accounting is just as it should be.

"How's business, Doctor?" Černý asked me as Klára and I were about to order drinks at the golf clubhouse bar. Černý that great-little Young Communist with the long prick who'd once threatened to demote me to Young Pioneer. That beardy poet. Now a partner in a business. And the unwritten godfather of the opposition. If anything approaching an opposition can ever be said to exist in Slovakia. Anyway, as Elena put it, he's cock No. 2 on our dunghill.

Šicko se šickim skapčano. Everything is connected to everything else.

"What'll you have? You know Nina, if I'm not mistaken, ha ha ha! But then it was basically you who thrust her into my arms, wasn't it? I actually owe my magnificent married life to you!"

So he hadn't forgotten…

He was laughing and began recounting the entire story about the sauna during our Young Communist League training course to his friends who were standing around us: Karol Todorovský, owner of several slaughterhouses and meat-packaging plants; Mikuláš Petrvalský, proprietor of a chain of drugstores and a member of parliament; and Demeter Tupý, a dealer in toys. Meanwhile their charming wives were eyeing up the latest collections of golf attire in the pro shop.

"Just fancy, he snatched a chick I was working on right from under my nose and dumped on me this harpy, who's never let go of me since."

He wasn't expecting any reaction. He ordered beers all round and nonchalantly bore the entire loaded tray to a table, so we all had to follow him.

"If it's your impression that he's carrying on as if he owns the place, then that's because he does…," I whispered to Klára in reply to the question she hadn't asked. "This club is the cherry on his imperial cake."

He noticed her.

"And where did this saviour of lost souls liberate you from? Though I reckon he's less interested in souls than in bodies, ha ha ha…"

"Cut that out, will you? Don't forget I nearly bopped you one once before," I retaliated in jocular kind. It worked. The jocular bit. His raucous laughter almost shook the clubhouse to its foundations and set the glass cases filled with golfing trophies jangling.

"That's great, Doc, great… I like you, I've always liked you!"

Suddenly his demeanour became earnest.

"How about this: for today you can partner my wife, and your lady friend and I will make another pair – but what's your name?" he asked, rising and taking Klára by the elbow to lead her across to the organisers' table and announce the pairings he'd just created.

"Do you know, I even had to teach him what *Spätlese* is? You don't know either? Right, this evening you must try one extraordinarily good vintage."

Jano Prcúch, the manager of Černý's golf club and his tournament administrator, scanned her fizog with its pouting lips and nodded his approval to me.

Nina and I were left at the table alone. She was still as freckly as a pointilliste portrait, but the neckline of her golf T-shirt with its three buttons spoke volumes in praise of the creativity of her plastic surgeon.

"Hi," she said.

"Hi… Quite a riot, isn't he? I expect you have no end of fun together," I said. There was no way of telling what she was thinking. The expression in her eyes was a total blank.

"You needn't worry about your Klára. He's not nearly as dangerous as he once was," she said. "You'll get her back undamaged without having to bop him one."

That was really quite funny and I tittered into my beer glass. She didn't raise so much as an eyebrow.

"Do you want to play with me?" I asked her.

"It's already been decided. This is *his* tournament and everything will be the way *he* wants it."

She blew out a puff of smoke. "Do you still do recitations?"

"Only on very special occasions nowadays," I replied.

"Today there could be one," she said, sipping her beer. "Today you can recite me a sonnet with eighteen lines." *Panem et circenses* ...

Suddenly a *fujara* started to trill, the French windows of the clubhouse flew wide open and, to a march played by a wind band, admitted a flock of geese and a dozen piglets. They strolled about among the tables and got tangled in the legs of the drinkers and they were followed in by some girls wearing branded lingerie and little cooks' caps and bearing more ingredients for the tournament dinner. Baskets full of eggs, pasta and Moravian potatoes, bowls of fruit, beautiful arrangements of fresh vegetables of every hue, nets bulging with glistening shellfish, huge chunks of chocolate, linen sacks of flour and sugar and, last but not least, four live eels and untold numbers of crabs clamped to various parts of the last model's body, making her look like a cross between Medusa and a stegosaurus. The cackling and grunting was drowned out by the applause that greeted Jano Prcúch when he opened the door to the kitchens and successfully drove the entire procession inside. There the animals found their final resting place, the girls – before they too might rest – heaps of jobs to do.

Černý was beaming. Now and again, dandy that he was, he would twist the end of his mega-whiskers round his *index finger*.

"While the grand supper is being prepared, which we are also expecting to be graced by the Prime Minister, we have to earn it. We shall now all head for the start, each to his own tee, and in exactly twenty minutes a pistol shot will signal the time for teeing off." He took a solid-looking piece from his belt and casually toyed with it for a moment. "Chop-chop, drink up and let's cross clubs, Doc!"

"Are you sure it's not dangerous? Has he got the safety catch on?" I shared my distrust with Nina.

"He never has it on," she replied. *Altius! Fortius! Citius!*

The competition went off as might have been expected. After teeing off our first ball, we and our golf cart ended up in the trees, Nina, without a word or the slightest change in her demeanour set about what was evidently her favourite activity – so far as I might judge from our previous encounters. She was good at golf and knew how to handle both club and balls. The buggy carrying Černý and Klára was one hole behind us and now and again loomed into sight, though that left Nina in no way disconcerted. It even struck me that when successive fairways met end to end she deliberately hit the ball so close that Černý and Klára couldn't fail to see us. If someone had filmed our progress from a distance and then screened it speeded up, but with all the actual golf bits edited out, the Keystone Cops would have blanched with envy.

We came away with quite a respectable score, though my driver was rather worn after eighteen holes.

A thought crossed my mind: This is his tournament, so has everything to be just as he wants it? *Mutantur omnia* *et nos mutamur in illis...*

A black-and-white slapstick comedy, that's it. Camera slightly jerky, exaggerated movements speeded up, 1920s ragtime, dialogues given in subtitles. Starring one swaggerer with a huge moustache, a potentate with a scowl, a gawky buffoon with a briefcase and two fateful beauties.

And the five fingers of a human hand.

The grand dinner began in style. During the day, the culinary wizards had converted all the fresh ingredients into an imaginative medley of flavours, colours, smells and consistencies. Just as they were bringing in, on huge trays, the pigs with golden oranges in their mouths, the Prime Minister also turned up. The swaggering Černý led him majestically to our table and we began to eat.

The PM, the Potentate, munching on a piece of pork. Close-up of that scowl.

"Doctor, I've heard you can read the genetic code."

The swaggerer Černý jokes that I'm a genetic cod and I take the Instrument and a syringe out of my briefcase.

"I'd need a drop of your blood, Prime Minister."

His bodyguards are by us in an instant, they surround our table and dislocate both my arms. The Prime Minister merely smiles benevolently.

"I can't let you have one; my genetic code is a state secret." The bodyguards roar with laughter and let go of me. "But could you read the code of this pig?" The Potentate makes a sweeping gesture, now he's drumming his *fingers* on the table. Close-up of the Clown, pleading written all over his face.

Subtitle: "It's never been tried on tissue that's been cooked, animal tissue at that, but in principle… If the Instrument can link up to the central genetic database, it might work."

Stirring music. I prepare a sample from a minute sliver of meat.

People at the tables nearby get up and press round us. The bodyguards have grown nervous. Todorovský, Petrvalský and

Tupý are standing right behind me. The Prime Minister summons the Minister of Agriculture, Kováčik, seated at the adjacent table, to join us. In next to no time the screen shows a sequence of numbers and finally an image of a little pink pig, the spitting image of the ones we'd seen that morning on their final saunter through the bar to the kitchens. The club buzzes and everyone claps. The Potentate claps me on the back.

"That's a Chinese pig," says the Minister of Agriculture, Kováčik. By now the subtitles are changing in rapid sequence.

"Chinese? What do you mean, Minister? That's impossible," says Černý, furiously waving his arms about. "The pigs we're eating came straight from our eco-farm at Hlohovec."

"No, we don't raise this strain in Slovakia," Kováčik insists. "It's a hybrid bred in China for the production of cheap meat, and we've made it illegal to import it."

Černý blanches.

"Look at these genetic mutations," the Minister points to the colour-coded groups of genes on the screen. (In the black-and-white version we see only various shades of grey.) "These are newly created and potentially dangerous genetic modifications. They may increase the production of meat, but there have been reports of increased carcinogenicity."

A ripple goes through the room, here and there someone squawks, and several of the guests head straight for the toilets.

Černý regains his self-control and declares: "Stay calm, please, there'll be a simple explanation for this. Prime Minister, sir, this must be some kind of conspiracy and you have my assurance that it will be properly investigated and things put right." He's lost his swagger, the Potentate just laughs: "Well, it seems to me that Minister Kováčik here will have plenty to investigate, and others too… Minister," he turns to Kováčik, "I believe that our agriculture, our farmers and consumers could well benefit from this… pioneering technology. What do you think, how many of the devices should we order from the doctor here?" He grins at Klára. "We have the best possible references for him, eh?" Klára smiles awkwardly and her eyes are like fragments of the Greenland ice-cap.

Nina, whose expression has been inscrutable ever since first thing and who has exhibited no emotion even during our criss-cross ride round the links, this sphinx-like face suddenly brightens.

"See, you've turned into a Pioneer after all!" she says.

PARVA leves cyfiunt animos ..

The band plays as people drink and chat about their good and bad shots that day and at previous tournaments. Černý has fallen silent and is drinking heavily. Todorovský, Petrvalský and Tupý are drinking with him. Borovička. Their charming wives are now eyeing up the collections of lingerie on display and sipping champagne, their *little fingers* sticking out like antennae.

"They've given approval for my treatment plant," says Todorovský, giving the *thumbs* up. "I've already spoken to Ďodi."

"All these things need is the right approach," Petrvalský declares.

"This time we won't get buggered about by the Minister," Tupý hammers it home. "No more of that you'll-have-to-wait lark."

"He's got to come to his senses, stupid prick," Petrvalský agrees and makes an obscene gesture with his *middle finger*.

As in any decent slapstick film, huge round cream gateaux are brought in. Tupý's wife can't resist: she tucks her *little finger* back, sticks out her *index finger* and scoops some whipped cream up from the edge of one. Tupý picks up a silver dessert fork and snappily spikes her *finger*, cream and all, to the wooden table top with it.

Their rings slip from their fingers, float off into the air then join together to form the shape of a golden heart. "Ah," the other guests sigh and begin to clap. "How much longer do I have to keep teaching you manners, cunt?" Tupý hisses in his wife's ear. The heart changes shape – now making a gold rhomboid. The guests go "Oo-oo-oo!!" and go back to what they were talking about before.

Semi-naked girls in a new collection of branded two- or one-piece lingerie bring round the coffee.

"I wonder if they haven't been modified as well," the Prime Minister jests, checking by hand to make sure. With *all five fingers.*

In a nutshell, everyone's having a fabulous time. Jano Prcúch offers me a cigarette. Pioneer, Young Comunist, Communist. Well, well. I'm feeling great. *Nam fuit ante Helenam cunnus taeterrima belli causa*

"I say, Doc, where d'you get that fancy chick?" Jano Prcúch whispers in my ear as he pours me out a glass of wine. He's only pretending to whisper, making sure Klára can also hear. "I've nothing like it in my entire collection, and that's saying something!" He winks at her.

I suddenly recall how much I'd wanted her that morning, but

have quite forgotten about it since. I place one *hand* on her thigh, patting her hot, delicate skin with my open *palm* and *four fingers*. I raise my glass, clink glasses with her and wink at her myself. Life is beginning to return to my groin. Again I can see the lighthouse blinking beneath her dress. I'm in for a wonderful night.

The black-and-white film acquires colours, all the objects in the club darken to a crimson-gold, like when the sun is setting, Rachmaninov is playing, someone seems to be reading, with pathos and unintelligibly, an archaic text; I hear the words Jonah, Armageddon, Lot. The camera retreats, on the horizon there's now some kind of Mesozoic sea monster with a long scaly tail, the whole club ends up inside its huge-toothed maw, and we're swimming around in it as in a lagoon surrounded by giant yellow canines, and the Titanic's funnels keep blithely churning out smoke.

Beneath the dangling white table cloth I feel her hand on my knee. It is making its way up the inner side of my thigh, higher and higher; cleverly managing my zip using two fingers, enclosing me in the palm and playing a special version of the Rachmaninov on my instrument with some original fingering. First, third, fourth – third fifth and second. And again, more slowly: first, third, fourth – third, fifth and … s-e-e-e-e-c-o-n-n-n-d. I have my work cut out not to start breathing too wildly. I am getting short-winded, I may have groaned, and when I feel a more sudden move I nearly come in time with the chord … but then the Prime Minister rises and begins to make his farewells …

"Good bye, Doctor, I'm glad to have made your acquaintance; you'll be hearing from my minister before very long."

I try to rise, but the tight grip isn't letting go. The pain of it causes me to let out a groan. Černý likewise, only his groan merges into an oath combining a reference to ladies of the night and the tool of their particular trade.

The Prime Minister lifts the table cloth and glances approvingly towards Klára. Beneath the surface, the translucent Greenland ice of her eyes has an edge as keen as diamond.

Černý's long member and my aching and still erect prick are tied in knots beneath the table…

Genesis

The Great Director was smiling. The Great Director was sniggering. The Great Director was laughing aloud as his hands patted his paunch. He was pleased with himself. From his little waistcoat pocket he withdrew a chalk and slowly, relishing every move, he chalked his massive long cue. He dropped a coin in the slot on the side of the huge pool table beneath a gigantic light canopy and pulled the lever. With a loud rattle the coloured balls came tumbling out. He weighed each in turn in his flabby hand, testing, with eyes closed, their temperature and inner vibrations, and slowly, savouring this moment of perfect creation, set them out on the green baize in utter contentment. Nodding his head, he then repositioned one or two of them, purring with satisfaction. Then he re-chalked his cue, made a final adjustment to the black and with one mighty friction shot he launched a cascade of collisions throughout the new galaxy.

Inter urinas et faeces

The ex-swaggerer Černý withdraws his revolver, but before he can decide which of the five of us at the table to aim at one of the security guys shoots him right in the middle of the forehead. His *index finger*, the one he spent the morning proudly twiddling his moustache with, that cocky *index finger* pulls the trigger in its final twitch, the gun fires and the bullet hits my Instrument. It's the last shot of his golf tournament.

Though by no means the last shot of the film. The real slapstick is only about to begin.

Todorovský, Petrvalský and Tupý immediately draw their own weapons and riddle the security guy with holes. The other members of the security detail return fire. And more of Černý's guests join in. A regular duel of *trigger fingers* ensues. Both camps overturn tables and keep up a barrage from behind them. Splinters of wood are flying everywhere.

For a moment silence descends as each side weighs up their strategy.

One of the security guards pops his bald head up over the edge of a table and ping! – a bullet parts his pate with a red streak. Intertitle: Splat!

Černý's lot try to surround the security men. Todorovský and Petrvalský are firing using both *hands*, bang, bang, baaang, baaang, and Tupý makes a dash for the next table. The guards spot him, rat-a-tat boom, but too late; only the dust flies up at his heels.

Someone at the back sets a fire and burning bottles start flying. Whoosh! Even the subtitle starts burning. Here and there an anti-tank round flashes through the air, Todorovský and Petrvalský having produced a bazooka from somewhere. The noise it makes ... yeeeow.

Tupý runs to another table that'll give him a line of fire to where the guards are more exposed. He manages to cut down three of them – boom-boom-boom – leaving their uniforms looking like sanitary towels after use. Intertitle: Aaaargh!

The guards reorganise the tables to form a barricade in the middle of the room.

There's a glorious smell of smoke, spent gunpowder, broken wood, spilled alcohol and blood. Boom, bang, rat-a-tat, peeng, thwack, weeee, whizzz, rata-a-ta-boom, zrrr, plip-plop-plip, wheesh ...

The girls wearing the lingerie collection join in, even the top-less ones. Tupý's wife disengages her *index finger* from the fork, licks the cream with its colour rinse of blood off it and starts thrusting away with it in terrifying style. Eeee-jab, Take that! Todorovský's and Petrvalský's wives quickly shed their outer garments and deftly swap their charming pink underwear for black stockings and bras. All three now arm themselves with silver dessert forks. Jano Prcúch gave a sign to the band, who strike up the theme tune from *Charlie's Angels*, Mrs Tupá takes the lead and the others caper behind her. The smoke-laden air is carved with arching somersaults, high heels and high-pitched squeals. Wheeee-shluck! Wheeee-shluck! The subtitles just can't keep pace.

It looks as if the guards' number is up. The tables protecting them are falling to bits. But what's going on now? Unbelievable!

Intoxicated by the scent of victory, Černý's lot start shooting with one *hand* only, pulling their erect members from their trousers with the other and showing them off to each other, comparing them for length. Todorovský and Petrvalský stop following the battle, toss their guns down and, quite unprotected, start masturbating with both *hands*. Oh-ee-ee! Shu-shu-shu! Shrieking wildly, they shoot their seed in every direction until a well-aimed or randomly flying bullet from the guards' side, or their own, cuts them down. Plop! They drop next to each other, still trying, in their respective death throes, to point their collapsing tent poles heavenwards. Seeing them, Tupý breaks cover, firing from all his toys at once, about fifty of them, like in a third world guerrilla catalogue, spinning round and round on the spot and looking like a firework display. Brrrrrrrrrrrrrrrm! He executes three quadruple Rittbergers, fires off some eighty rounds, only to be downed by a single one, which fells him right there alongside his companions.

The security guards are well-trained and probably lack pricks worthy of being shown off. Alone the Potentate stands high on a pyramid of overturned tables, gripping in both *hands* his massive dong with a flag attached, which he waves undaunted over the heads of the combatants. Shiny silvery shreds descend from the ceiling and land on it like snowflakes.

The Černý side, now rudderless, begin making themselves scarce. Some, acting as if nothing at all is going on, carry on drinking from broken glasses. Jano Prcúch is chatting away in his dusty, bloodied suit until, wearing a broad, forced smile and repeatedly bowing in the direction of the Prime Minster, he makes to retire from the scene. From behind some of the barricades the odd empty or, heaven forfend! – full bottles still occasionally come flying, along with plates, bowls, chairs and eventually, obviously, cream gateaux. But the Prime Minister's guards finally eliminate even these last pockets of resistance. The last things left flying about are just curses, but then everything falls silent.

With one deft swipe the Prime Minister slices off Černý's black moustache, which he then glues painstakingly to his own upper lip. And finally, with some flair he catches the last flying gateau and holding it aloft on the five *fingers* of his upraised *hand* declares:

"The war is over. The people of this land have prevailed. We have sunk the unsinkable. On the ruins of the old, rotten, destroyed order we shall now construct a new, better and more just society. A society where the rich will not be against the poor, the well-fed against the starving, and all against the government! A society where, on the contrary, the rich, the poor, the well-fed and the starving will live in concord and love their government!"

The subtitle soon spread across the entire screen and began to reproduce asexually at an alarming rate.

The people of this land have prevailed.

We have sunk the unsinkable.

On the ruins of the old, rotten, destroyed order we shall now construct a new, better and more just society. A society where the rich will not be against the poor, the well-fed against the starving, and all against the government! A society where, on the contrary, the rich, the poor, the well-fed and the starving will live in concord and love their government!

The people of this land have prevailed we have sunk the unsinkable on the ruins of the old rotten destroyed order we shall now

144

construct a new better and more just society a society where the rich will not be against the poorthewell-fedagainst thestarvingall againstthegovernmentasocietywhereonthe contrarytherichthe poorthewell-fedandthestarvingwillliveinconcordandlovetheir-government!

All will live in concord and love their government!

Love their government!

Government!

All!

We set our table back on its legs, sat down on our rickety chairs and in concord tucked into that last gateau with our bare *hands* until the police and press arrived. It was excellent. Pure chocolate. I had just stuffed my mouth full of it when I spotted someone taking a photo of me.

It was Elena.

"You've got some lovely brown smudges on your face. It'll make a brilliant photo to go with an article about you. I know what I'm going to call it: '*Inter faeces*.'"

It wasn't a subtitle, or a speech bubble; it was her actual voice.

Blinded by the camera flash I could just make out that she was giving me the *finger*. I couldn't tell which one.

But it wasn't her *ring finger*, m'lud.

The end.

Vulgarisms... Too much to my taste.

They didn't bother him. He, my husband, didn't see the point of them. Too much energy, too many emotions. Squandered seed, like with masturbation.

One time I brought a book of poems by a young woman. They struck me as fresh, genuine, not least of all because they didn't avoid such words, using them to identify her real feelings. With no self-censorship. They weren't vulgarisms. It was nudity, true passion, passionate truth, and quite unglossed. And at the same time defiance, true female rebellion.

He just sneered with a snort of dismissal. "In the whole of Heller, and he's full of passion, realism and truth, there's only one vulgar word. But it chimes," he said.

What if *I* were to write a book? About him perhaps. What kind of words would I use?

But then, what do I know about him? What had there been before I showed up? I'd have to make things up. What did his rancour stem from? Who'd hurt him, and how? Who was it who turned him into the monster I'd been living with? Was there a woman involved?

And I have started making things up. It must have been a gorgeous aristocrat, or artist, probably both in one, and she'd repulsed him and so dented his self-esteem. Hence the way he shunned others. To live with me – non-aristocratic, non-artistic me.

I probably don't have it in me to produce a book. Literature. "Art". Like that wretched Patient, my husband's favourite Colleague. Post-traumatic stress disorder, secondary asthenic depressive syndrome with toxicogenous hallucinations and suicidal tendencies. My husband's diagnosis had been sound. Or he was being too kind to him. Clearly, he'd been a schizophrenic. No syndrome. A mental case. I wonder if he pulled his suicide off in the end?

If this "Gaudeamus" was meant to be literature, "a work of art", I'd have stopped reading it long before this. I couldn't care less about all those perversions, his fascination with the lexicon of the lavatory, his perverted obsession with explicit details. Only a genuinely sick individual could write like that.

Or someone determined to disgust the reader. Perhaps to conduct him, like Dante, through all the circles of Hell so that he might pass through purgatory on the way to Paradise? Mm, I don't think so... After all, this isn't a book intended to be read.

The vulgarisms aren't the problem here. My husband taught me that there's a place in literature for all the means that a language has at its disposal. *Homo sum, humani nihil a me alienum puto*. I remember we once had a discussion about pornography. "The vagina," he said, "is the only thing on which men and women agree, and people have turned that single agreeable topic into a taboo. The fact that people don't talk about the vagina in its own right, that all talk of intercourse, passion, or sex is tinged with crimson shades of raciness and sin, that we're not taught at school how to recognise and apply appropriate emotions and vocabulary, all this leads to superficiality, frustration and humbug and creates the space for pornography and criminality."

(Yes, that's what he said, with six 'ands' in a single sentence...)

Thus did my own vagina become an object of ratiocination and scientific enquiry...

Or aesthetic analysis at best.

Heigh-ho...

So I shall read this "Gaudeamus" thing to the end.

What *have* my musings brought me to?

What has my vagina got to do with the story of that girl?

Šicko so šickim skapčano? Everything is connected to everything else?

VITA BREVIS
Ars autem longa

Right then…

I was in my hotel room and really should have been celebrating. It could have been a great day for business.

But I was in a cage and neither a visit to Ľudka at the cemetery, nor the recollection of Lucia's body in the hotel mirror were of any help.

So… suicide?

I listened to Ravel's *Tzigane* on my headphones.

Music… The perfect way to express emotion. No wasted words, no superfluous descriptions, or explanations. Thought converted into sound. The undulation of molecules in space. One motif, another, the interplay of sorrow and determination, dance, the language of the body. Dissonance, stridency, chaos, a glorious struggle for existence. Where's that motif gone? Has it died, got lost? Will it be reborn? Is there anyone else here? Yes, someone is entering, barely perceptibly – a third motif? It gradually absorbs the cacophony and weaves it into a tune. Is it *joy*? Silence … ! And here it comes, like fresh out of a bandbox, like a newborn cleansed of blood and sebum, like a lion-king standing proud above the savannah – a victory dance of a crystalline purity.

Music and the arts have learned that a message passed from man to man through the medium of art cannot be put into words. That for the expression of feeling a completely white, untainted canvas may suffice. Or a chunk of rock or iron, a pile of gravel. A calligraphic inscription is not saying the words written. The inscription embodies all the history, pain, *joy* and experience of hundreds of generations, the myriad destinies of men, women, children and old people.

Words are weighed down by meaning, their specific content as set out in dictionaries. Precisely because they are precise, they are incapable of capturing an essence. There are poets who liberate words from their sense. They string them together in new constructions, testing to see if they might not give rise to a new wind to turn the wheels of the cosmos.

For anyone to understand a heap of gravel, or a snow-white canvas, they must allow the dominant feeling of existence – sorrow – to silence the jolly, breezy funster they like to play at being for want of any better idea, and then open up the minuscule dermal valves, those millions of tiny pores, on his face, the palms of his hands, his shoulders, thighs, abdomen, hair, everywhere … And sorrow like a warm, cathartic tsunami can then flow into his skin and nerves and veins and brain – yes, that's it, that's us, that's me …

Words …

How am I to express my feelings through words? How can it be done without it sounding banal, trivial, hackneyed, kitschy? How can I formulate such an ordinary thing – I was sixteen and in love with a girl, I loved her for the thousand days until they killed her, I was left alone, half a living organism, a one-legged jumper, the square root of two, 1.4142135623731, yes, I'm more than one but less than two, they left me the 0.4142135623731 of you, but I'm missing the other 0.5857864376269, awkward though it is to put it that way, but then not even mathematics is exact; Pythagoras was wrong: not even the abscissa that meet in a perfect right angle can accurately determine the length of the hypotenuse because the universe is crooked, oh yes, so very, very bent. I MISS YOU!!!!!!!!! It's much as if when they killed you, that 0.5857864376269 of me also died. Not even Kirchhoff's first law applies! What is left of our two currents that entered the node of that wretched night?

It has been enough for me to live, breathe, eat, enjoy success. But then man is said to exploit only ten per cent of his potential. So I live. What else is left to me … ? *Amore more re* …

Yes, we should have been celebrating. It had been a great day for business.

I should have phoned Lucia.

She'd have been there even before I had time to open a fresh bottle.

"You'd rather be dead?" she'd have said.

She'd have caught me by the hand and dragged me out into the corridor. We'd have dashed up the hotel stairs. Her supple legs would have taken the stairs two at a time, with me panting along behind her.

"Where are you t- … ?" I'd have asked, unable to finish the question, and she wouldn't have taken any notice anyway. We'd have run up to the top floor. She'd have opened the small iron door with its coat of grey paint and we'd have gone out onto the roof.

As far as I could, I would have held the air in my lungs. We'd have been in the midst of a glorious spectacle of light. Above us the stars, beneath us, all the way round, the living-breathing city. The yellow lines of the streets with the red streaks of the traffic, the irregularly lit rectangles of tower blocks with their mosaic of windows, the seemingly silent and unobtrusive houses of the wealthy, the dark patches of parks, the mirror of the river, the floodlit Castle.

"You know the tale of the turtle", Lucia would say, "swimming in the ocean and once in a long while surfacing to take breath. A rubber ring is floating on the ocean's surface. The probability of our being born is the same as the probability that the turtle will stick its head through the ring as it comes up for breath. We've all succeeded though. We've surfaced through the rubber ring. We are the club of lottery winners, that incredible band of the lucky ones."

Luck, *just a stroke of luck* …

Do I really want to die? Do I want to hand the jackpot back? She'd have grabbed me by the hand and walked over to the edge of the roof. We'd have stood between that teeming of loan winners and the eternal history of matter.

We'd have both taken a deep breath and kicked off together. Mother Earth would have embraced us with the force of her gravity. We'd have remembered our forgotten mother tongue. Kids gone astray returning from Babel to her embrace. *Dust thou art and unto dust shalt thou return.*

The wind in our faces would have been ever so gentle and warm.

"Make a wish!"

What do I long for? What would I wish for except peace and death?

"Remember what you were like. Remember the things you used to like. Remember who you are!"

Shortly before, at the cemetery… that's when I'd been myself. Or not? I'd wept, pleaded for forgiveness, longed to make a change. Really? Or, from the safety of my shell, had I merely been snivelling at the cameras of the cosmos about the bad hand I'd been dealt and begging for another sweetie.

The soft maternal embrace beneath us was getting closer. In it there are no agonising questions, no reprehension, just warmth and peace.

A word might have sufficed. A single word.

And the Word was…

Mm, He… Of course, this is the moment when He can't be overlooked.

Eli, Eli, lama sabachthani?

Who forsook whom, and who is the forsaken one?

Who is to return to whom? We to the Mountain, or the Mountain to us?

"Make up your mind. It's time. Will you return your gift because don't you know what to do with it, or will you accept it and try again, this time for real?"

Socrates would have said:

"The hour of departure has arrived, and we go our ways – I to die, and you to live. Which is better God only knows."

So… So such are we…

Koyannisqatsi.

Samsara.

Nos habebit humus, nemini parcetur.

We spend our entire life dying. We spend our life committing ritual suicide. Only through the perfect ritual of hara-kiri can the samurai preserve his honour.

Honour.

In the end I decided:

"*Stand to the last.*"

There are more important things to life than death. The only way of avoiding death is to live. *Per aspera ad astra!*

A dark giant of cumulus clouds lowering over the Little Carpathians, resting on the silhouette of the horizon, would slowly squeeze through, flashing its eyes. Then it would let out a weary roar – like a lion expected to perform his circus act yet again.

The wheels of the cosmos would go into reverse, the bungee cord would stop momentarily, we would feel the hot breath of death on our faces, Earth's tentacles would miss us by a whisker

and immediately the vast accumulation of energy would fling
us back among the stars.

Was it then? No, further back than that.
Like a meteor I fell towards thy lap
and missed thy world by an inch,
a world in which love's pinch
causes all with pain to flinch.
So now I'm going back as from the start of time:
Naked and pure, and yet to reach my prime.

Eli, Eli, lema sabachthani!

This controversial Aramaic cry given out by Jesus Christ as he was about to die was often repeated by my husband, and even in Slovak...

"God, why hast Thou forsaken me," I would hear coming from the bathroom as he was shaving, or when he had reached the end of some long armchair rumination by the fire. No, it wasn't a sign of piety; he never prayed. We didn't go to church, priests were people he avoided. He never talked about God, except when remembering his Colleague.

"No one yearned more for God than he did," he would repeat.

He was a great one for negation, the more the merrier... *Nemo, nunquam, nihil...* Three categorical negatives in a row, that was typical.

"No one would have got on so well with God as he would. No one could have a better appreciation of the depth their mutual understanding, the protophysical inevitability of that disposition, Never could anyone have evinced greater empathy with the dialectic of the fragility of the equilibrium of His work."

So many of's in a row, that was also typical.

"But God wasn't interested in being understood by him, which constitutes proof of the invalidity of the hypothesis of His existence," he concluded.

Thinking about it now, I'm unclear as to whether he was speaking for his Colleague, or himself. Most likely they were in agreement: If God does exist, He doesn't understand their language, He doesn't do logic-based riddle-solving, and so He's not in the club.

That I wasn't in the club either was entirely a matter of course.

Pium Desiderium

Everyone you meet leaves his imprint on you.
A signature in your autograph book.
The peaks and troughs of the bas-relief of your karma.
A shuffling of the cards – the nucleotides of your DNA.

I never made Kamil's photos into an album, but I did take them everywhere with me in a large packet. The black-and-white ones had started to yellow slightly, and the coloured ones... oh dear, as the photos had become things of the past, so too had their colours.

I was sitting on the bed, going through the photographs.

At the bottom of the packet I also found the slides, wrapped in fine tissue paper.

Histology mounts.

Bits of Ľudka's body.

How could I have forgotten… Oh dear, what if…?

I hastily switched on The Instrument. Černý's bullet had left a big hole in it, but the display had survived unharmed. Would it work? I scraped a fragment of the dried tissue from one mount and mixed it with a tiny quantity of saline.

A few surviving DNA molecules should suffice.

All the processes came up on the display as usual.

Or did they?

Persona non grata

From out of the fog of digits and patterns the lineaments of a naked human body gradually took shape. But the Instrument wasn't behaving as at other times. The image sharpened to an unbelievably true likeness and at one moment even began to undulate in such a way that the facial features became three-dimensional.

But it wasn't Ľudka's face.

The body had been a man's.

I recognised the face. It was Raffal's.

Raffal was one of the seven men guilty of Ľudka's murder. He'd been the one who had finally held her harrowed little head under the water until she stopped twitching. And it was his mother who, at the Palace of Justice, would have had me believe that Ľudka was still alive.

Suddenly his body stepped out of The Instrument and Mr Raffal, MSc, the murderer of my Ľudka, was standing there in my hotel room, naked.

"Good evening," he said, adding: "Excuse me," as he tried awkwardly to conceal his nakedness.

Mechanically I tossed him the hotel's bath towel.

Among all my emotions, all the questions I had, I suddenly didn't know what to say first.

"Pleased to meet you," he said, attempting to overcome his embarrassment. What's there to say to that?

"You're …," I stammered, "a murderer …?"

Of course I knew that not everyone was convinced that he was. Despite repeated appraisals by a number of judges, despite his confession to the murder, some people still harboured doubts. There was even a theory that all seven had fallen victim to a monstrous communist conspiracy.

Suddenly it dawned.

"That's the proof! Irrefutable evidence at last! Your DNA on Ľudka's body. Your… sperm …," I groaned in agony.

"That's not clear-cut," he objected. "There were several of us …"

"That's irrelevant, you wretch," I retorted, forgetting that I was addressing an apparition. I wanted to hurl myself at him and strangle him.

"Go on," I rasped instead. "Go on, tell me what happened. How could you do such a terrible thing?"

"How was I to know it was a terrible thing?"

"What? Murdering someone? Don't you know that taking the life of a nineteen-year-old girl, a girl who is the most beautiful thing in all Creation, a girl who brought *joy* to all who met her, you don't know that that's a crime???"

"She didn't bring me any *joy*."

He was worse than I'd imagined. He was a monster.

"Evil?" he asked, probably reading my thoughts. "What is Evil?

And what is Good? How can one tell them apart?" The chimera, hologram, avatar or whatever it was seemed abstracted. It was staring right through me into the distance.

"How was I to know she was any different? She was like other chicks. Miniskirt up to her backside, tight-fitting top, sexy perfume, make-up… there are thousands like her. All just ripe for the picking. Pulling one's easier than peeling a banana."

"This banana hadn't wanted you to peel it. Is that why you killed her?"

"It's how the world's made up. Some peel bananas, some are bananas and some are just peels. No one said it was murder."

"What, for God's sake?"

"Eating a banana. Bunches of bananas, plantations of bananas, primeval forests of bananas. Falls of lambs, flocks of ducks, shoals of sardines…"

Either The Instrument wasn't working normally, which it obviously wasn't, or, no less obviously, this man, or whatever it was, was mad.

"Get on with it, then, what did actually happen?" My patience was beginning to run out. "How did you drown her?"

"Dunno," he said. "I wasn't there."

"What? Where weren't you?"

"I wasn't there when she drowned."

"How so? A minute ago you confessed to murdering her. Oh, I see, I forgot you're a great one for making confessions then retracting them," I couldn't resist the jibe, though it did occur to me that it was a pretty silly thing to say in the circumstances.

"Murder has many faces. I didn't know, it's not written anywhere, and it's not taught at school. I've had twenty-four years in jail to get the hang of it. He who kills isn't always the one who squeezes the throat."

He looked me in the eye.

"And you?" he asked.

"What about me?"

"You've never committed a crime?"

The conversation was getting nowhere. Černý's bullet had done something to The Instrument, something which is doubtless full of potential, but what it was churning out at the moment made no sense.

"I wasn't there. I could have done it," he went on, "but I didn't. If I had been there, maybe I would have done it. Possibly. But I wasn't there."

"Where weren't you? And where were you? And how come you're here?"

"I'm inside her memory. She remembers me. I asked her to dance. She turned me down. I wasn't used to that. Girls would go with me with never a word of protest. I'd got a car, money, … And if ever one of them started on about her mum by the time I got to taking her panties off, it was too late. Either she'd be brought round with alcohol, or…" He fell silent.

"Nobody's going to let their life be ruined for the sake of just one bird. Life is a project in which everything has to fit together neatly. Deadlines, money, people. A project has to work, a project is more important than truth, than men, than life. At a given moment every project becomes a crime."

"What *are* you on about, life is a project and a project is more important than life? Dammit man, did you kill her or not? What happened after she turned you down?"

"I killed her, for sure. All crimes, great and small, finally lead to murder. I've killed your Ľudmila many times during my lifetime. I've killed millions of Ľudmilas. I know now."

He looked at me one last time.

"And you?"

"What about me?"

He made no reply. His body became translucent, lost its three-dimensionality and broke up into a plethora of numbers and patterns on The Instrument's display.

Dunno…

I got my first slap around the age of eleven. When our football broke our neighour Mr Sabol's downstairs window. He nabbed whoever he could and called the police. The policeman asked me who did it, twice he asked. The first time I answered that I didn't know.

The worst punishment in our house was to be sent into the corner. The bigger boys from our block would sometimes nick my hockey stick or marbles, or they might trip me up as I roller-skated past them, or they might just say: "What are you starin' at, d'you wanna thump?" until I learned never to look them in the eye.

Ivo Paják, a boy from school who lived two stops further from school than I did, always tried to stop me getting off the bus until I burst into tears or flew into a rage, which gave him as much pleasure as tearing the legs off a cockchafer or hurling a frog down onto concrete and counting the times it came round.

One time I was surrounded by some Gypsies as I was on the way to a piano lesson; back then they still lived in the city, three of them, boys like me. We had a brief scrap, my music flew out of my bag and ended scattered across the wet pavement like the posters they used to throw from planes on May Day. Just as they'd appeared they vanished, I gathered up my scores and went on to my lesson.

But I'd never been slapped in the face. So when I suddenly felt the back of the policeman's hand because of that broken window, I was terrified and feared for my life. I spilled the beans. The whole beans. That the ball had been kicked by Milan, and where he lived.

I don't know... If the policeman had stuck needles behind my finger nails, if he'd held me under water until my lungs nearly burst, if he'd threatened to shoot me if I didn't confess, I might well have said anything just to have him let go of me and leave me alone. Maybe if he'd hinted that my mates had said that the ball had been kicked by me, I'd have told him it was them, and if he'd hit me again and wanted to hear that we'd all kicked the ball together, deliberately, because we didn't like Mr Sabol, because he kept taking our ball, so we'd *meant* to break his window and that we hadn't actually wanted to break just the window, but that ghastly old head that never stopped shouting at us from the window, we'd wanted to knock his block off and silence it once and for all, have it fly off his neck to the dustbins where it would have been found by rats and stray dogs, I'd probably have spilled the beans just to avoid been hit again.

After all, it would have been no more or less true than what I did say. Milan hadn't even been out that day. Milan never played football with us.

So... Maybe, maybe. I don't know; I only felt the back of his hand once.

In Memoriam

I took the histology mounts and quickly scraped another sample off. I waited. But Raffal didn't come back. Instead The Instrument spewed out the naked body of First Lieutenant Solčáni.

"Goodness, what are you doing here!? Ľudka can't have known you, could she?"

He replied just as soon as he realised where he was and who he was talking to.

"We did meet. I investigated a slight... a slight accident that she had..."

Accident? I knew of no such thing.

"You remember, she wrote to you about it. In one of the letters you passed to me. One evening when she'd wanted to revise, one of her girlfriends talked her into going for a glass of wine at a hotel. That night, one man, quite important in his day, fell in love with her. Whether it was by chance, or whether he'd spotted her previously, I failed to discover. At any event, it was a hotel that people like that used to use for chance pick-ups. It was the hotel where you and I last met."

God almighty! The hotel where Prcúch ran his training courses for the Young Communists. The hotel where I first met Černý and his wife, the hotel where I'd first tasted the pleasures reserved for the elect.

"Oh, right, I remember. I had a splitting head…"

"Well, that time there was a certain, let's say incident…"

"She never told me," I voiced my scepticism.

"She was a very brave girl, she had guts. There was only one thing she feared – losing you," First Lieutenant Solčáni told me.

It was May and the trees, flowers and birds were organising their most boisterous orgies. Plants tried to outdo one another in gaudiness, shapeliness and the powerful emanations of their sexual organs. The air was filled with a heady scent and pollen.

After six weeks I couldn't wait a minute longer and I took her the minute we closed the door of my little room. It was over in no time. She looked at me, watching. She seemed a little pale, tired, after her journey? I've felt that look again since – coming like a living photograph from the repository of time – its colour, warmth and light, which landed on my retina like a sticker on an Easter egg.

There's something in that look that confuses me. At the time I didn't worry about it. I was happy, the waiting had ended, I had her there, to myself, in the flesh, no mere dreamed-up memory, no mere prayed-for envelopes glinting from inside my mailbox, I desired nothing else, just to hold her in my arms, fasten onto her with my every pore, breathe in her scent, listen to her breathing, feel her heart beating, sink into her liberating embrace. I could tell that she understood my impatience, I could see the wisdom and the deep love with which she tended me and smoothed away my tension. But was I also seeing in her dark green eyes a happy, joyful longing? Or – somewhere deep within – pain, humiliation and fear?

Oh, God, my love, how could I have failed to spot it – something

was troubling you. What was it? What did you not want to tell me?
What were you keeping from me?
What had they done to you? *Pater*
incertus

"What did they do to her?" I went at Solčáni.

"Power is ruthless. Power arrogates to itself as natural, just and inalienable the right to have anything it wants. And believes that it can take it at any time, by force if necessary. The man in question made a mistake. Ľudka was the stronger of the two. She wasn't afraid of him. She told me about his threats as if they were nothing to do with her. She was quite clear about it. It wasn't that she didn't see the danger, but that she thought it irrelevant to what she deemed right.

By contrast, it was clear to me that a life was at stake.

Possibly two lives ..."

It's going to need some software tweaking to get these fantasmagorical beings coming out of my shot-through Instrument to stick to the point and speak out clearly and intelligibly, I thought. What two lives was he on about?

"When power is at stake," Solčáni went on, "life is no obstacle. And it doesn't matter whether it's one life or two thousand, nine hundred and seventy-seven lives or sixty million lives." He was beginning to sound like Raffal.

"Just what happened though?" I roared at him.

He looked at me as if he was finally sorry for me, but he just went on.

"All we had was her statement and I was ordered to stop the investigation. But then there was her murder to deal with and obviously there was no avoiding that line. Except I couldn't complete that investigation either."

"Is that why you committed suicide?"

He smiled imperceptibly. As if through the eternity of Time he could see all the futility of worlds.

"Of course …," he said, "of course it was suicide … One hundred per cent suicide …"

"Hence the two lives …"

"My life isn't important, we can discount it. You see," he took a deep breath, "at that hotel … there was drug-taking. What I mean is that that night Ľudka wasn't fully conscious the entire time …"

"Hang on, what do you mean? That *night*?"

"I'm a bit confused, the post mortem didn't confirm it, but Ľudka told me she thought she'd been …"

He began to break up on me.

"Hell! What are you trying to tell me? Are you implying …? I have to know, wait!"

He was gone.

Respice
Adspice
Prospice!

I grabbed a slide, meaning to scrape off another sample. Then I jibbed.

Who'd come out of The Instrument this time? What if it's …

Over the years I'd become inured to the idea of seven young men whose party mood got the better of them and who, drunk, lost all their inhibitions and any respect for life. My enmity had gradually dispersed and changed into disdain and ultimately pity. By murdering Ľudka they had murdered any prospect of a happy life for themselves and their nearest and dearest, irrespective of whether they were found out and officially punished or not.

But for any encounter with the mysterious, influential man of whom Solčáni had spoken I was quite unprepared. For a moment or so I turned the slide over and over in my hand before setting it aside and switching The Instrument off. I took several deep breaths and walked up and down the hotel room, smoking a cigarette. I ordered another bottle of champagne. Then I cancelled the order and had a bottle of whisky instead. I was trying to digest what I'd just been hearing.

"There were several of us…"

"How was I to know it was a crime?"

"Murder has many faces."

"All crimes, great and small, finally lead to murder."

"The autopsy didn't confirm it, but Ľudka had been…"

What in Hell's name could an autopsy confirm two months after the party was over?

Had been…? My mind refused to finish the sentence.

But the autopsy hadn't confirmed it…

The trouble with you is that you believe everything you're told. You know what a smarty-pants Solčáni was, how he always knew everything and everything was clear to him, just calm down…

Calm down? How can anyone think that I can be calm?

Once again I peered back through the mists of time into Ľudka's eyes, which were trying to tell me something.

I swigged the whisky straight from the bottle as if that's where the answer lay.

Suddenly it dawned.

De profundis

It was I who had murdered Ľudmila. *I* was the most execrable, most despicable and most pitiable criminal. I, who was supposed to have loved Ľudka, I, who should have been by her side, I, who should have been her protector, I hadn't lifted a finger to save her. I hadn't given even half a thought to the possibility that she might be in trouble, that she might need my help. I had failed to read in her weary eyes, in her uncertain movements, in her touch that sought comfort and relief, anything of what was troubling her. I'd been thinking only of myself, *my* needs, *my* blind desire to have her. Yes, that was it, to possess her, I had used my power, the fact that she loved me, to bind her with my demands so tightly that she'd been afraid to tell me that she was in danger, that she was afraid, that she was, dear God, so very, very frightened. She had believed that she would manage, cope with everything, as she always had, alone, unaided even by me. Instead of saving her I had cast her, that summer's night, into mortal peril, it was I who'd come to Bratislava, I who'd held open the door of her kidnappers' car and bowed: Here you are, sir, here is your victim, she suspects nothing since she was brought here by me, I've made her ready, don't worry, she trusts me, she's yours, man, have fun with her, do whatever you want with her, whatever you desire…

And then, what happened later when you didn't arrive in Košice? Did I get on the first train and go in search of you? Did I stop and ask every passer-by if they'd seen my Ľudka, if they'd help me find my Ľudka? Tell me, people, what's happened. Did she get into trouble, has someone harmed her? Did I scour the Earth, did I turn the heavens upside down to shake the truth out of them? Not a bit of it! I wallowed in my grief, consoled myself with my loss, prided myself on the uniqueness of my suffering.

Death divided us. I lived on like a scorned, abandoned lover and you ceased to exist.

And I didn't protect you, not even when they were hurting you, and they did hurt you, repeatedly and for such a long time. Your name has become a symbol of ineptitude and callous injustice, and anyone has been able to do whatever they liked with your body. Those who had it in their power to restore to your name that which belonged to it – beauty and love – and to your ashes peace, couldn't be bothered and I merely looked on and said nothing and went on living this narcissistic life of mine.

If ever I were to write a book about it all, it too would be all me, me, me…

I'd have the plural in the title at least. "We" sounds better than "I".

Pluralis Maiestatis …

We, the people of Slovakia, mindful of the cultural heritage of our forebears…

We the peoples of the United Nations, determined to save succeeding generations…

We, men of Athens…

We want nothing foreign, we shall not cede what is ours!

We're not like them!

Who is not with us is against us!

We want peace!

We want a goal!

We, King Bright Sun…

So such are we…

"I."

"We."

Especially when attributing blame:

Who killed Ľudmila?

(Or might not "They" be better?)

Gaudeamus igitur

I glanced at The Instrument. And took a massive swig from the bottle.

Now you're close to me. Closer than you've ever been. Please, I beg you, for the third time tonight, forgive me. Despite everything I have loved you, loved you to the best of my ability. I know that you loved me too and that you never spoke of your suffering because you didn't want to lose me. Which may be exactly why you did lose me.

Let's not make the same mistake twice. Speak, I beg you, speak to me. Please do… Please!

I switched The Instrument back on and prepared another sample from the slide.

I waited.

The Instrument was working ever so slightly slower than normal, possibly because of Černý's bullet hole. For a long time I could see nothing, just a mass of numbers. The patterns started coming much later. Sometimes the screen gave a flash, some sudden discharge. The Instrument worked on, but with an odd crackling sound and beginning to overheat. Though that was the least odd thing that evening.

Finally it came up.

What came tripping out of the screen were children. Little ones, bigger ones, toddlers, school kids, teenagers, boys, girls. They all looked like Ľudka and they all looked like me.

There were sixteen of them.

The tiny ones started crawling all over me, a little two-year-old girl snuggled into my arms, a slightly older boy perched on my head, others hung round my neck or tugged at my hand. The oldest ones came and sat round me, saying not a word and smiling.

They were our beautiful offspring.

In the middle of that bleak hotel room, in the middle of that lost city, in the middle of a stolen country, in the middle of a hopeless universe, there was I, a happy father, surrounded by my children.

I was crying and laughing at one and the same time.

Then I began telling a tale.

Once upon a time there was a king who met the most beautiful princess in the world. Their wonderful wedding, which went on for a long time, was attended by good people from every land. The king and queen had sixteen children, stalwart princes and golden-locked, wise princesses who, when they were grown up, went out into the wide world to make it a better place.

Before leaving, they came to say good-bye to their parents. They sat in a circle round the throne and the king said:

"You, my children, were born to us as the most handsome

princes and the most beautiful princesses. You have learned all the wisdom of the world and your hearts are undaunted. But to make the world a better place needs something else as well. Beauty, wisdom and valour alone cannot vanquish evil, stupidity and cowardice. Before you go, let me give you one more gift that will assist you," he said, and handed out sixteen little boxes, one each.

"Take great care of these gifts. They have a magical power. Use it with care even if your human powers fail you. If the need arises, you won't even need to open the boxes; the gift will come to your aid by itself.

"And now, children, you may go…"

Long after they had disappeared I sat there motionless. In my arms I still held the invisible baby. My mind was blank. I sensed only their presence, I felt only their touch, I could hear only their movements.

When they abduct and kill your girlfriend, when for five whole years no one can discover who did it and then they tell you that they'd drowned her and that before drowning her they'd raped her several times over, and that there were seven of them and that they'd be tried and convicted and then they'd be let back out and then they'd be tried again and then say that it hadn't been them and that what had actually happened wasn't known, and never would be known, then going mad is the most normal, the most sensible thing that you can do.

O, laugh, ye laughers!
O, mock now, ye mockers!
Ye who laugh verily and snicker so merrily,
o, laugh and chortle as you will!
O, crow and cachinnate – the mirth of mockingful mockers!
O, scoff till your sides split, the mirth of scoffingful scoffers!
Laughingly, laughingly,
chuckle and chortle,
snigger and titter,
jeerers, sneerers.
O, laugh, ye laughers!
O, mock now, ye mockers!

Alter ego

In the large mirror in which I used to see Lucia's curves I now saw only myself, sitting on the edge of the bed, old and wizened, my big eyes shining and terrified, my long, useless arms dangling from my sunken shoulders, the bottle in my paralysed hand held at an angle and trickling the viscid, costly whisky onto the hotel carpet.

So… you're writing a book?

Why? What's bothering you, what do you really want?

(Lucia was forever asking: Who are you and what do you want?)

Do you want to be like the wise and all-powerful King Solomon, and to describe an innocent girl from the vineyards, the beautiful and flawless Sulamith, who, like Ľudka, carried through the night the flower of her love and devotion, heedless of the snares of a wicked world?

Do you want to drink dry the cup of love like Tristan and his Isolde and never sober up until the end of your days?

Do you want to forget the rest and live only for your Helen, like Paris?

Do you want to give up on the world and give up yourself like Faust because of Marguerite?

Do you want your heart to come back to life like Onegin's because of Tatyana?

Do you want, like Odysseus after all his travails, to return to your Penelope who is waiting faithfully for you?

Do you want to be like Peter and die along with your Lucia amid a global cataclysm?

Do you want to go mad because of the world like Hamlet and forget all about your Ophelia?

Or do you want to come to terms with your loss like Andrej with the loss of María?

Or do you want lay bare your breast, your bleeding heart and alter destiny, change the rules of the world? Do you want to descend to the underworld like Orpheus and win back your Eurydice, or to free Ludmila and your native land from evil like Ruslan?

Do Truth and Love have to prevail over lies and hatred?

In the same mirror I could also see that pale young man with eyes like dead coals who I used to look at after a night on the tiles way back during that training course with the Young Communists. It was like meeting another lost son. I had an urge to hug him.

"D'you know what? Keep all those saccharine displays of love to yourself," he said without warning. "Look at yourself! Who do you want to fool with your pathetic ramblings? Probably only yourself. Or Ľudka? You know that won't work. And anyway – who's the whole thing supposed to be about? Juliet? Or just Romeo?"

He didn't seem thrilled by our encounter. "'S obvious, look: Ta-da, a paragon of sensitivity! Your romantic Hollywood hero is as much like your real self as a May Day parade is like real socialism. You're just a callous, arrogant, hedonistic opportunist. You'd have no scruples about taking the battery out of a kid's toy and sticking it in your vibrator! You'd swap anything for a moment's gratification."

I wasn't prepared for a talk like this. Truth to tell, it knocked the stuffing out of me. I took a swig of the whisky.

"But this isn't about gratification… Do try and understand. What comfort can there be for an injured soul? We went through it together, didn't we?" I said, turning to the old guy as if I were looking for an ally of my own generation. "They took our love from us, they took our ideals and in the end they took our character."

"Oh, an 'injured soul', ha bloody ha! What do you know about suffering? Your suffering boils down to not knowing which number in your diary to call tonight and what to choose from the menu."

They showed me no mercy.

"Character! What is it, that 'Noble Character' of yours? You wake up in the morning as a Noble Character. You brush your teeth, have a crap, put your tie on as a Noble Character. You smile like a noble Character. You're above it all. You may even pause to think about how to save mankind. But it only takes ten minutes in a medium-sized shopping centre, or in a bus, or in the doctor's waiting room and your Noble Character is a goner. Everyone keeps pushing into you, treading on your gleaming shoes, crumpling your new suit, breathing their germs all over you, daubing their sweat on you – and you start wishing you had a machine gun. You look about you, you see your fellowmen, those hapless wretches, bald petty bureaucrats with their leather briefcases clamped to their chests, anaemic, bleary-eyed mothers pushing before them their prams bearing future criminals, sixteen-stone teenagers stuffing themselves with popcorn, their gaze vacant and their ears blocked with headphones, filthy, brain-dead characters bin-diving for used syringes, supercilious matrons with an opinion on everything and wrinkly boobs crammed into their low neck-lines, successful idiots with gelled up hair running the globe via their mobile phones – you look on and start thinking of genocide. So don't come the Noble Character with me!"

"Can't you just leave me alone?" I begged them. "Do you have to start poking about in that stuff right now? I want to be left alone with my memories."

For a brief moment we were all silent. But only a moment. The old Dorian Gray in the mirror just wouldn't let up.

"You don't have to summon up your memories with The Instrument. Your sodding memories are right here, any one of them could, at any moment, leap out from some dark corner."

"Yeah, let's go for it, it could be quite a lark," said the young Dorian and came and sat closer. He was speaking in low tones, seductively, so much so that it felt like I was whispering into my own face.

"Let's remember one more time our great pal Julo Černý, may he rest in peace. Do you remember him telling us that you are and ever would be just a piffling little Pioneer?"

"I think I acted with particular heroism on that occasion, didn't I?"

"But that was the last time. And anyway it was only because he'd touched a sore spot. Your conscience and your unbounded ego."

"My ego! I'd always wanted to be the best, that's all."

"Really? You've never wanted to be the best, you only wanted to seem like the best. Like that time at Mrs Lejko's, remember? Or to the parents of your patients. Remember how Samko's mother blamed you after you'd told her that her third child was also dead. Enjoy one last time the look in her eyes, red from weeping, all the world's acrimony focussed on your damn white coat, her look as it tried to pierce your armour-plated immunity like a wooden stake piercing the heart of a vampire."

"That's not fair as well you know. Samko and his brothers had an incurable condition. But then – you know full well how it was."

"Yes, let's remember that too, why not? But wait. Dr Iwannabethebest, our Mr Loser, Mr Nobody has run up against Mephistopheles, who promises that he'll no longer be Mr Nobody, but that henceforth he'll be Mr Somebody! Let us relish the

Quidquid latine dictum sit altum videtur

shame, let us again be carried away with the knowledge of how brilliantly it's working out! Make a wish and they'll all line up, all your friends, all those jerks with broad grins and deep pockets, you can shake hands with them again and wish one another many more boom times together. You sold our soul, Dr Faust. And for what?"

I had to have another slug of whisky.

"You're crazy!" I told them. What else can you tell your own image in a mirror, especially when there's two of them?

Tertium datur

Gagarin's question runs thus:

A young person with his whole life ahead of him should

A: - have himself fired into space and then try to conquer it with his smile?

or

B: - encapsulate his experience of life in the words of Karel Kryl's *Unknown Soldier*: Piss off, right, piss off!

Quo vadis?

"I have tried. Honest. All my life I've tried to be a person of character. Whenever possible…"

"Maybe there *is* nothing like the true human Character," someone else said suddenly. "Maybe there's only the Brain, reacting to the situation around it."

I couldn't be sure how many of those images I was actually seeing. There were two Dorians in the mirror, so there must be two of me too, so four in all… Or six, eight? Or even more? I had another swig instead. The whisky was a good one. Genuine Scotch. Fifteen years old.

"Exactly so! I've been trying to tell you that for ages, Bro. Brain. It's the Brain that's the swine. It knows exactly what to come up with when. What manoeuvre, what trick, what strategy." That was another one, No. 5?

The situation was getting very confused. They started trying to outshout one another. Everyone wanted to have their say. Suddenly the room was full of them. Voices coming from every direction.

"But it's all just down to chemistry!"

"Euphoria!!"

"Civility, pretence!"

"Deception, malice, hatred, aggression…"

"Kindness, empathy, sincerity, the odd smile!"

"*Joy*!"

(*Joy* – the daughter from Elysium…)

"We're all just chemical formulae, chemical reactions! Electrons changing orbit, molecules that arise and perish."

"There's nothing to be done about it!"

"A matrix."

"Silence!" I shouted and the din stopped for a second.

"As regards my character, the deeds I do and what I will do, it's me who decides," I declared, confirming my determination with another hefty swig. It really was good. Pure peat.

"Unfortunately," said the young Dorian.

"No chemical reactions! No molecules!" I tried to insist, another swig.

"Really? Are you sure?" There was no holding these clever-Dick Dorians back. No let-up.

Ad Hominem...

"D'you think it's you holding the reins?"

"Can you still keep a grip on anything?"

"Okay, you do the deciding. Right? Good – so now decide. Think about it."

"Think! Ha, ha! Tell me what thinking is."

"What's your decision-making really like? Huh? And where does it happen?"

"The thinking or the deciding?"

"Now you're getting me confused. That's all you ever do."

"We ought to be focussing on the essence."

"That's right. At last we're getting down to brass tacks…"

"Get on with it, this is getting on my nerves."

"That's probably because they're made of sh*t!"

"You take a good look at yourself instead, at all the bits of *you* made of sh*t!"

"Gentlemen, gentlemen… Language!"

"Have you heard they've started performing shit transplants?"

"Shit?"

"Transplants?"

"Transplants."

"What else might you have expected? How else could it have ended?"

"Nothing's ended. We're still at the beginning."

"Are you sure?"

"Where were we?"

"Trying to get you thinking. Now!"

"Now what?"

"You be quiet. We're doing science. When we get onto sex, you can come back in."

"Jews have big cocks."

"What???"

"Yep. Big ones, they really do."

"You've got shagging on the brain!"

"No, honest, you'll see! It's definitely the Jews behind everything."

"Rings a bell. My inner voice!"

"Inside your brain."

"What d'you mean, inside my brain?"

"That's where thinking happens."

"Bingo!"

"Paranoia, voices, delusions… It doesn't need a psychiatrist to tell what's wrong with you."

"Like I said, it's all down to chemistry. Didn't I say that? Didn't I? I did!"

"And have we eaten anything yet this evening? And why do we have to be sorting all this out now?"

"No, but I did say so, didn't I?"

"I don't know who started this, but can't we cut it short? I know, let's bring Lucia in."

"Why Lucia, for goodness' sake? Surely Elena. We need to wind this up with Elena."

"No, Tanya! We ought to wind it up with Tanya. Rather than…"

"Huh, 'wind it up', right?"

"Come on, let's try and agree…"

"Agree? With you around? I'd rather wipe my mouth with sh*t!"

"You don't have to. It's like you've always used sh*t for lipstick!

And plastered your whole sh*tty face with it!"

"If you're thinking that the more vulgarisms you use, the greater conviction you'll carry, then you're wrong, you stupid prick!"

"Are you sure?"

"Jews and money. That's pretty much the same thing."

"I'm off. You can tell me later how it ended."

"This *is* the end. Right here and now. We're done."

"And d'you know why?"

"Why what?"

"Or the Jews!"

"Or exercise books."

"Meaning?"

"The ones you stole. They brought you to Slobberyenot and Černý. And they've got plenty. Whole cupboardsful. You could have played battleships and noughts-and-crosses with them."

"The Great Head, that's you! It's you who's the Great Head, isn't it obvious?"

"Are you quite … ?"

"And now tell us the truth, pal: If you'd been there, would you have done it?"

"How can you live with it?"

"And the PM an' all! Lest it be forgotten …" 0 *Tempora!*
0 *Mores!*

"So? Do you think you can change anything? That thanks to some notion of your will, of your – forgive the expression – Noble Character, something's going to change? That you'll write a book and they'll all shit themselves? For God's sake! Do you seriously think that anyone's going to be interested in any crap you churn out? Or that today anyone gives a toss for Sládkovič and his 'two great loves', his beloved Marína and his no less beloved Slovakia? Nemo, nunquam. Nihil!"

"Just be sure to put in all the women you've had it off with and how. That's what they like hearing about. You'll be able to sell the film rights to Hollywood."

"And you have to be cool."

"Like I said, rise above it all."

"No truth. None of that Noble Character stuff."

"What if it turned out you're gay?"

"Or that you were abused as a child by your own mother!"

"Along with your mentally handicapped brother."

"Oh, yeah!"

"You disgust me. Thoroughly disgust me. Doesn't your own dignity matter to you?"

"But that's the point. Nothing matters!"

"Ennyvay ze vind blowz ..."

"Just get it into your head that you can't change a thing. Everything's given, calculated in advance like an eclipse of the sun; the entire future and entire past of the cosmos has been expressed once and for all, it's irrevocable and unalterable. For all those hundreds of millions of years when dinosaurs ruled the Earth it was clear that the day would come, one quite specific date, when, out of the blue, they would all die out. There is no freedom of choice. No options. No Gagarin question. Nothing."

"Listen up, Bro. You're a loser, a swine, but you're innocent. Your Brain, your Ego, is no more than the executor of the eternal cosmic will. In an automatic, sophisticated and effective way it gets on with its filthy task. You're just a pre-programmed robot."

The old man in the mirror, having listened to all this, rose and said slowly:

"I don't think you should drink so much." *Communicutur est...*

I scrutinised all those impish figures one by one. Never before had we looked each other in the eye. Yes, things needed putting right. I too stood up, if a little unsteadily.

"You're right. Things have gone too far. We've messed an awful lot up. We've done an awful lot of harm. Now leave me alone.

I took another swig. The last. It really was a good whisky. Bloody good. I tossed the empty into a corner.

… As things are, life is nothing but a desperate attempt to kill time somehow, to find some way to keep our brain cells busy, to stop them getting bored…

… All right, you've had your fun thinking stuff up, so now pack your bags…

I grabbed my Instrument with both hands and dashed it with all the force at my command against the mirror.

Game over, hasta la vista, bye-bye!

The shredded fragments of Dorians went flying across the room, shrieking like Angry Birds playing Ludo. Several shards struck me, but I felt no pain. By this stage I was feeling nothing at all.

What had expanded had now contracted. My swing had stopped swinging.

Lorem ipsum

"Neque porro quisquam est qui dolorem ipsum quia dolor sit amet, consectetur, adipisci velit…"

Lorem ipsum dolor sit amet, consectetur adipiscing elit. Proin condimentum, mi eu efficitur sodales, arcu orci eleifend ligula, sed rutrum libero lectus a tellus. Sed suscipit risus sed eros pretium, vel posuere augue faucibus. Donec malesuada, quam vitae lobortis semper, nisl metus pretium nisl, ut eleifend risus tellus nec nisi. Praesent vestibulum turpis neque, ac varius erat fermentum ac. Maecenas vel vestibulum velit. Ut ultricies lobortis. Proin dapibus arcu a ornare pretium. Proin vitae arcu dui.

Cras ut ultricies ligula. Vivamus et libero lacinia, ornare nunc vitae, vehicular ex. Vestibulum eu ornare nisl. Etiam laoreet imperdiet interdum. Aliquam non tortor placerat, faucibus ipsum a, dignissim diam. Nullam condimentum et tortor ac faucibus. Sed sollicitudin, nulla finibus accumsam veneatis, augue erat ullamcorper justo, eget mattis eros odio et massa. Aliquam scelerisque elementum tortor eu posuere. Pellentesque habitant morbid tristique senectus et netus et malesuada fames ac turpis egestas. Etiam elementum magna sit amet consequat malesuada. Curabitur laoreet, tortor et sodales hendrerit urna nunc sodales tortor, ac rutrum dolor metus et metus. Curabitur nec libero et ante fringilla efficitur sodales laoreet metus.

Donec nisi sem, tristique non enim at, finibus faucibus purus. Cras a dolor purus. Sed porta tortor id dolor tempor facilisis. Class patent taciti sociosqu ad litora torquent per conubia nostra, per inceptos himenaeos. Aliquam nec porttitor felis. Vivamus arcu quam, imperdiet eget risus sit amet, placerat tempor risus. Sed vitae odio ultrices, pulvinar mauris sed, voluptat felis. Proin felis diam, maximus sed scelerisque at, pulvinar sed eros.

Quisque sapien dui, rutrum vel porttitor in, sagittis ut velit. Nullam vehicular ac mi sit amet tincidunt. Morbi eget laoreet enim. Proin in lorem velit. In sed magna elit. Aeneam luctus pretium gravida. Morbi metus dolor, mattis at faucibus sit amet, rhoncus non mi. Quisque dignissim tristique enim, id dictum nisl venenatis eget. Curabitur nec porta dui, in dignissim velit. Fusce commodo, arcu eu vehicular interdum, lectus sapien euismod lacus, et finibus turpis ipsum ut urna. Nunc mollis pellentesque urna sed finibus. Donec eget maximus nibh. Nullam vulputate libero a lacus gravida imperdiet. Cras facilisis, ante vitae varius feugiat, velit edi eleifend dui, ut molestie sapien eros non ipsum.

Nam convallis blandit ante. Vivamus laoreet blandit nibh a mattis.

Nullam ipsum nulla, blandit in sollicitudin non, faucibus nec ante. Sed nibh quam, ornare ac posuere non, varius vel turpis. Donec placerat purus sapien, ultrices tristique leo rutrum vel. Suspendisse in ultrices odio. Sed metus urna, iaculis sed tincidunt sit amet, feugiat pellentesque lectus. Nunc ultricies fermentum mi ut euismod. Donec aliquot, neque eu condimentum accumsan, urna tellus consectetur erat, vel interdum felis libero vitae metus. Praesent rhoncus sollicitudin quam, non rhoncus nisl elementum at.

Nunc
et in hora
mortis nostrae

So in the end we had met. After all those formalities with the tunnel, the lights, the gateway…

My thoughts were as burdensome as Sisyphean boulders. Shards of the broken mirror were still flying past my head and in them I tried to fathom out where I was. I was feeling like a boxer after a knockout. I felt sick. As from a distance I could hear the referee counting me out.

One, two, three…

The room was a cross between a room in a hall of residence and a student flat. In the corner was an unmade bed, with various items of clothing tossed onto the crumpled duvets. Old manuscripts were tumbling out of the cupboard, and, crammed together like the knots in a Persian carpet, an infinity of artefacts of various historical and geographical provenance filled every inch of the walls. The air reeked of tobacco smoke and an elusive mix of perfumes and spices.

Sitting at a large table like judges, robed in academicals and wearing wigs, were three men and a woman.

Her Majesty the Professor.

So these are the ones to judge my Noble Character, it dawned on me. The glass fragments had begun to fit back together.

Four, five…

The Great Director was sitting on a round chair running on eight castors, his vast frame squeezed into a tight-fitting shirt, over which he wore a waistcoat with a fine checked pattern. Flickering on the wall opposite him were millions of tiny screens like parti-coloured fish scales.

Flashes of eternity.

"That wasn't bad, eh? What do you think?" He had swivelled his chair round to face me. He was neither old, nor young: he looked like those ageless bachelors who never have to shave and of whom you're not quite sure whether something isn't wrong with their hormones, or whether – heaven forbid – they might not have inherited some genetic disorder.

He took a drag on his hookah and passed its mouthpiece to me.

He fished out a bottle of wine and two glasses. He withdrew the cork, took a sniff with his eyes closed and poured out.

"Try that. 1582 vintage, one of the very best."

He was right. It was… divine.

"Us'll stick wi' borovička, gents, if you don't mind," said the first of the academics, oddly in dialect.

"1956 vintage, the overall best," said the second. They all burst out laughing.

"Your health! Cheers!" That was the third, winding it up.

"I say boss, do you have any of those cheap fags left?"

The Great Director opened a new pack and gave them a light each.

"So show me, how've you developed?" said Her Majesty. She undid my flies and I briefly felt her cold hand on my testicles. CSE, I recalled. She bent her wrinkled face down to me and whispered as she continued kneading me: "Very good, you've turned out well!" She pulled me over to the huge billiard table in the middle of the room, hitched up her skirts and lay down on the green baize. The greying, crumpled skin on her abdomen and thighs was laid bare before me, the folds of fat hanging over the edge of the table. She thrust me between her splayed legs, grabbed my buttocks with both hands and kept pushing until she yelped like a cat at midnight.

Six, seven, eight...

Goodness knows what this summation of my life's achievements should be called. It began to dawn.

My life is a sanitary towel, a used condom cast into the dust.

The Great Director was slowly sipping his wine and puffing at the hookah. I went over to him and asked:

"Is this all? This... is it all?"

The academics finished their cigarettes, armed themselves with billiard cues and tried shooting the black between Her Majesty's wide-open thighs.

The Great Director poured me another glass of that divine

wine. He selected two fat Havana cigars from a humidor.

"And what did you expect? A pat on the back? Satisfaction? Forgiveness?" He gave a threefold laugh. "Ha, ha, ha!" He handed me one of the cigars, carefully cut the end off the other one and lit it. He blew the smoke right into my face.

Nine, ten.

The mirror was back together, Sisyphus had reached the top.

"I want to know what happened! I want to know the truth! Why did you do it? Why did you take her from me? Tell me at last where she is!" I shouted at him.

This time he gave a fivefold laugh.

"The truth? What is truth?" he asked with indifference, as if he'd lost interest in me. He stood up, leaving the space on the chair with its eight castors vacant.

"Do you want a go? Try it. It's a game fit for the gods! Do whatever combinations you like, go on."

He sat me at the control panel, fitted me with headphones, and a code of some kind popped up on the monitor.

"Now you can begin. You can take destiny into your hands, as the saying goes. Ha, ha, ha, ha, ha, ha, ha!" Sevenfold.

Cui prodest?!

The Great Director extended his right arm with the cigar between his fingers towards the monitors. From each miniature screen on the wall rays of golden light flashed towards his hand. With a rapid flicking motion he caught them like flies, held them for a moment and then opened his hand to me like a thimblerigger.

It held a coin.

"Ecce! Voilà! Ha!" he said. He handed it to me.

It was simultaneously as hot as a freshly roasted chestnut and cold as an icicle. Golden as the sunlight, but also silver like the hair of old men, green as the northern lights, blue as the sky in summer, white as fresh milk, black as the night, pink as a newborn and red, yes, red as blood. It smelled like the sea, like a meadow in spring, or soil after rain, like a bride before her wedding night. Its surface was slightly shiny, but on closer inspection I could see into it as into the depths of a mountain lake. And in the depths everything was moving. Depending on how I tilted the coin I could see pairs of eyes, an infinite number of human eyes. Some were laughing, others were sad, some frightened, others weeping, and some were just tired and vacant.

The Great Director took the coin back and, slick as a football referee, flicked it high in the air. He caught it, turned it onto the back of his other hand, saw which side was up, and, cigar between his teeth, walked over to the billiard table. Her Majesty and the other three quit their fun and games and handed him a cue. He slipped the coin in the slot and pulled the lever. With a great rattling noise fifteen spanking new coloured balls rolled up from the bowels of the table.

From his fob he took a cube of blue chalk. Slowly, savouring every movement, he systematically chalked the tip of his cue.

Through the smoke of his Havana cigar he started singing, quietly and a bit off-key, that old student hymn:

Gaudeamus igitur
Juvenes dum sumus;
Post iucundam iuventutem,

Post molestam senectutem
Nos habebit humus.

Vita nostra brevis est,
Brevi finietur;
Venit mors velociter,
Rapit nos atrociter;
Nemini parcetur.

Ubi sint qui ante nos
In mundo fuere?
Vadite ad superos,
Transite in inferos.

Ubi iam? – Fuere.

So let us rejoice while we are young; after an agreeable youth, after a bothersome old age, the earth shall have us.

Our life is brief, it will shortly end; death comes quickly, cruelly it siezes us; no one is spared.

Where are those who were before us in the world? You may ascend to the heavens above, you may cross down into Hell.

Where are they now? – They have been.

The coloured balls flew in every direction like atoms of a new universe. Her Majesty and the three men in academicals, glasses of borovička in their hands, solemnly joined in:

Vivat academia!
Vivant professores!

Long live academe! Long live professors!

Piss off, right, piss off!
I turned back to the controls.

෨

At this point there was a piece of paper slipped inside my husband's Colleague's book.

I still had a clear recollection of my husband's handwriting from the days when I used to help him in the surgery. That perfectionism of the old fogey that he'd become… Words set down like the eggs of an autistic hen on perfectly lined paper, all the letters perfectly formed, all the t's crossed and i's dotted.

I am afraid that I'll be born again.

... And forget everything I've ever learned. I shall sit again on that tail of the COMET and ride on it — from one end of the Universe to the other... (playing with fire and ice and thinking how wonderful it is to have the solar wind whip the comet's hair across my face)...

... until after many, many light years of charging hither and yon, I understand once more and again that the ideal condition for every particle of my body and soul is ZERO.

ZERO energy, ZERO mass, ZERO thoughts, ZERO obligations, ZERO expectations!

Zero is the ideal number. Zero constitutes the whole world. Only if we split it into plus and minus do we get chaos and suffering. The sum of total of everything at both the beginning and the end is... ZERO!

Anything you win → you'll lose.
Anything you find → they'll take from you.
However often you succeed → you will spoil something — just as often.
Anything in between is a
WASTE OF EFFORT.!!!

Aha. So, Gaudeamus... Let us rejoice...

This note and the Latin tags in the margins... it's almost as if he'd been putting them in a book of his own.

199

Deus
ex machina

There was a knock at the door of my hotel room.

I didn't recognise him immediately. The crow's feet round his eyes had deepened, but his rascally face fungus was still the same.

"Corporal! Where did you spring from?" I gave my old army pal a hug. "What's going on? What's the time?"

Huck looked at his watch.

"Hurry up, Doc! You caused quite a to-do at that bash of Černý's. There's all sorts going on. Come on. We have to go, I'll explain everything on the way." Like all Czechs who've lived a long time in Slovakia he spoke his own unique hybrid version of Czechoslovakian.

He switched on the television. The news was on non-stop, the Prime Minister's brief speech about defeating the forces of destruction and exploitation was followed by shots from various cities, pronouncements from various important people and photos of the Prime Minister with Černý's whiskers, towering over the golf club ruins and waving his massive prick with the flag on the end.

"People are going to wake tomorrow to find themselves in an unfree country. The PM is assuming absolute power. But I refuse to serve any more bastards. We've got to beat it out of here."

"Hang on, Huck! You might have your reasons for 'beating it out of here', but what made you think of me and where are you taking me? I might have a couple of things here that I'd like to see through first," I protested.

"I have to show you something. There's no one on duty at the secret service archive today." *Et Tu, Brute .*

We got into his car and in no time he was tapping out the secret entry code by the main gate.

"So, Huck, you were a secret agent in the army?"

"Yep. I was there because of you. You probably never noticed, but you've been under surveillance all your life. Hang on and I'll show you why."

We traipsed along dark corridors – at least it struck me as traipsing, but Huck was striding purposefully towards a goal known only to him. I clutched at his shoulder from behind.

"Why should I trust you? That whole year I treated you as a friend, but you were having me on the entire time. You swore at the commie bastards, you sang piss-taking Russian songs with us, and you made trouble in Marxism classes. How am I supposed to know what you're up to now? How am I to know whether or not you intend to dispose of me while the country's in chaos or what will become of me, if you don't just toss me in the Danube?"

"Hurry up, Doc, we haven't got much time. Give me just one minute."

Exactly one minute later I was holding in my hands the very thing we'd come for. It was the service file of a secret service agent. Its first page bore the name Marina Shihab Sa'dia. Beneath it was a photo of a woman of about forty.

Despite the poor light, the woman's years and her hijab, there could be no doubt: the face was Ľudka's. *Fiat lux!*

The start date of her collaboration exactly matched the date of her death.

Code name: Agar.

Status: Sleeper.

Assigned to: Air base H3.

Huck quickly gathered up various dossiers and put them in his bag.

"Huck," I said. I was holding the document in front of me and staring fixedly at the photo.

"Huck, she … is she alive?"

"I don't know, Doc, I don't know… Come one, quick! We'll go there and see."

I followed him in a daze. Outside there were lots of soldiers and flashing blue, red and orange lights. The road was lined with newly hung, bewhiskered portraits of the Prime Minister. Crowds had begun to gather. What was intriguing was that both the supporters and the opponents of the Prime Minister were carrying the same triumphant photo with the flag. Only the wording on the banners was slightly different. "Now we'll teach you a lesson!" "Your P with a capital P", "Whose turn is it today?" and "Slovakia has risen!" as opposed to "Our strength and our hope!", "Flagpole of hope, flagstaff of victory, bright sun of the future!" and "Slovakia has risen!".

In the squares songs were being sung, pints pulled and paper plates of sausages and mustard handed out. The mustard was hot, the sausages nice and fresh, the beer cold, the songs heroic, optimistic. All as it should be. Spirits were high. Everything had been forgotten, everything could start afresh.

Huck drove me off to some place where we got out. We passed through perhaps six checkpoints. At each Huck flashed his badge; he'd slipped me one too, so I held out my hand automatically, the soldiers saluted and let us pass.

We were at an air base.

We boarded a small plane parked there. Huck donned the headphones, I did likewise and we belted up.

He started the engines. In no time at all we were leaving Slovakia's air space.

He handed me the bag of documents.

"Start reading. You'll find the time passes quicker."

Day began to break.

It was getting bright very quickly. We were flying in the direction of the Earth's rotation, in step with time.

Soon we'd have more light on the subject.

Ad acta

I rifled through the papers. Mostly they were just annual reports on the situation at the base.

Ľudka's handwriting… Her lovely little rounded letters with a slight lean, letters that had joined up to make words of love in my letters, but here they made up cold, alien, meaningless sentences.

"What's a sleeper?" I asked Huck.

"Someone who leads a normal life at his appointed place, usually with a change of identity; they don't have a specific task except to wait. When the need arises, a task will be given them. Perhaps after thirty years, perhaps never."

Here it was. *Change of identity.*

They hadn't altered her date of birth.

Planted in a friendly country in the Middle East.

Accommodated at air base H3.

Contact with home country: nil.

Means of communication: nil.

Situation reports: once a year.

Delivery of reports: by special courier.

Password: "Gaudeamus".

(How poetic, I thought…)

Memorandum of cooperation… provision of information on the running of the air base, attitudes among the men and civilian staff…

Movement about the base: unrestricted (except for communications facilities).

Movement outside the area of the base: strictly forbidden.

Next document: *Order to take on an agent.*

Annexe: *Agar action plan.*

Isolation of target. No communications, in the event of any immi-nent risk of cover being blown, action to be taken at once.

PECCAVI...

I had to stop. My heart was pounding somewhere high up in my throat like a frightened mouse trapped in a corner.

"Corporal," I said in due course, slowly and quietly. "What sort of people *are* you? What have you done? You... you pretended to be my friend and you knew... and you said nothing, for a whole year...!"

"I didn't know, Doc... My task was to keep tabs on you. I wrote down what you did, what we talked about, what you like, who you met, what you thought about. That's all. What was behind it all I only found out much, much later.

"Do you remember Krůta, the counter-intelligence guy? He knew something. He wanted to enlist you in the secret service, they wanted to do something about you. Some people wanted to tell you, you'd have been deployed somewhere together, but you buggered it up, Doc. You were a dead loss... The only things you didn't blab about were things you didn't know... And let's be frank, he didn't like the way you made a cuckold of Vančík. You were an unacceptable risk."

We fell silent. What Huck had said... the idea that all those years Ľudka and I could have been living together somewhere... that on that fateful night when I was grubbing about in the putrid innards of Monika Vančík I'd frittered away the chance of sparing my Ľudka any more suffering... the idea was unbearable.

After a while Huck went on:

"Never in my life, Doc, have I met anything so bloody vile as this. Never in my pretty shitty life have I ever known anyone to have been so totally buggered about like she was. Those years at the base, in the middle of the desert, with no news from home … I just can't imagine it.

"D'you know what H3 is? Thirty planes, sixty pilots, support staff, their families and nothing else. No shop, no cinema, just desert and enough food to eat, a mosque and accommodation blocks. The nearest village is sixty kilometres away."

I read some more reports about life on the base. Dull, dreary reading.

One of the first ones ended with a formal request: "I request some photos from my previous life." Stamped "GRANTED", with the handwritten addition: "10 max."

My mind travelled back to Kamil and how we'd developed them.

So. So…

Orbis pictus

The land beneath us began to change. High mountains, their peaks covered in glaciers, green forests, fields neatly divided into tiny squares and rectangles.

Wherever we flew, we could see, in the courtyards of palaces and castles, emperors, presidents, kings, heads of government and ministers. Out of the glittering glass buildings of great companies and banks came governors, chairmen, general managers and trade-union leaders, in villages it was their mayors and the chairmen of residents associations and parish councils, crawling out from their barracks and bunkers came commanding officers and from hospitals their directors and senior consultants, while outside ordinary houses, detached or multi-occupancy, stood the heads of families. Bands were playing everywhere, people in gaily coloured costumes sang stirring songs in various languages about their native lands and triumphing over the enemy. Everyone wore a smile, everyone waved to us.

Though from that height you couldn't tell what with.

The whole Earth beneath us was teeming, tiny people everywhere. We had glimpses even into their living rooms where they were beating their wives, and the bedrooms where they forced them into having sex. We saw mothers maltreating their kids and kids murdering their parents. The landscape was crisscrossed by little silver streams and great golden rivers. People were drinking from them, bathing in them, throwing rubbish and puking and defecating into them. Around them they were building dams, stone walls and military defence works. They prayed to them and stole them along channels dug underground. As they did so they kept a furtive eye on us, occasionally smiling guiltily, now and then brandishing their little fists at us, then carrying on where they'd left off. All this went on in a kind of idyllic harmony, which seemed barely ruffled at all by our presence.

Ant VIVERS aut MORI!

The towns and villages were replaced by the steely flat of the surface of the sea, then by a narrow green strip of coastline and then nothing but the endless grey-yellow of sands.

"I say, Doc," Huck broke in as he piloted the plane. "You should appreciate that it's quite possible that they'll shoot us on landing. I've no idea what it's like at the base now. Our latest intelligence ends with the report you're holding, and that's from several years back. The situation in the country is confused, the army's divided, and some parts are controlled by local militias. Kidnappings and murders are commonplace, and if they demand a ransom for us, obviously no one's going to pay. The moment we land, this plane and our lives are theirs to do what they will with."

He reached into his inside pocket. "I've got papers here for both of us and enough money to be able to fly on to somewhere else and start a new life there. That might be worth thinking about. So think about it…"

I glanced at the instrument panel.

"We'll be starting our descent in three minutes, Doc. Unless you take a different view, we're going to land."

I closed my eyes. I was suddenly overcome with fatigue. I hadn't slept in twenty-four hours. I remembered Spružina, Černý, the PM and Elena, Klára, Nina and Lucia. I recalled my entire life since Ľudka's death. Or disappearance, as it had transpired.

You have been spared all this chaos, Ľudka. Amid the roar of planes and the endlessly shifting sands you've… who's to say… have you perhaps found your spot of happiness?

Death… Only a while previously I'd been thinking about it. Actually the previous evening. But this morning, now, now I wanted to live. Now I wanted to see her again. See… and perhaps take her in my arms… if she'd let me. Just listen to her if she was minded to say anything. Just keep silent if she meant to stay silent.

Ruslan and Ludmila crossed my mind. I'm coming to save you from the evil Chernomor. I'll slice off his beard and we can go home. My sweet Ľudmila.

Suddenly it seemed impossible, nay, improper, to wish to

'liberate' her and take her away with me. Where to? I have no better option for you, my love. The world is an amazing place, full of beauty and poetry. But beauty has venom in its eyes and poetry wears a mask concealing the features of a murderer.

Ceterum censeo...

So such are we, my dear. Two stars in the cosmos, two flowers on the cold earth, two diamonds in the desert.

Do you think it would be possible for me also to find my smidgen of happiness here, at your side?

Do you think that you might be able to… save me?

You are the one fixed point in my universe.

Or must I, like Ruslan, deliver a city from its enemies first? Defeat the Hydra and cleanse the Augean stables like Hercules?

I will help destroy dissolute Troy. I will outsmart the Cyclops, I will pass safely between Scylla and Charybdis. I will resist the sweetness of the lotus, the call of the Siren and the offer of immortality in the embrace of Calypso.

Are you still waiting for me, my Penelope?

No, I'm not Ruslan, or Hercules, or Odysseus. I'm neither Saul, nor Paul and I have no right to be preaching a new observance.

I'm just that tall, thin lad with long hair watching out for you at Košice station on a Saturday morning, bleary-eyed from waiting and longing.

Dum Spiro Spero!

"What I have been living till now, it hasn't been life," I replied to Huck. "If they shoot me, I'll have lost nothing. You destroyed my life when you took Ľudka from me. If she'd been alive I'd have been someone completely different."

"You might have been the same buffoon, Doc."

For the first time since we left the hotel our eyes met. We started laughing and couldn't stop.

"I'm descending for the approach, Doc," he said blithely.

"Huck," I began gravely. "I think the time has come for me to put my parachute training to the test. You've got a parachute around somewhere, haven't you?"

"Don't even think about it, Doc. You don't have a chance, alone against that lot!"

"Quite the opposite, I reckon. If I jump beyond the area of the base and show up on foot, I think I'd have a better chance than if we landed right under their noses. Not to mention the likelihood of them shooting us down first.

"There's no point the two of us showing up, Corporal. When I'm going on a date I don't need anyone to play gooseberry."

"But they aren't going to understand a word you tell them," he continued to raise objections.

"All I'll take with me is this," I said, tearing out of the file the page with Ľudka's photo on it. "If she's there, they can't fail to recognise her. If she's not, there'll probably be someone who remembers her."

"I owe this to you, Doc. I owe it to both of you."

"You've paid your debt, Corporal."

"Okay, Doc, as you will." He took a little box from his pocket. "Here… when you meet up with her, this might come in handy…"

A magic box?

A ring. A gorgeous gold ring with a constellation of tiny diamonds…

He'd thought of everything.

"Thank you, Huck Finn. If she says yes, I'll come and find you. Even now I'm looking forward to your best man's speech. But don't go raking up any titbits from our time in Olomouc!"

I donned the parachute. Below us the desert was bisected by the road leading to the air base. Straight as a die.

Stand to the last.

Gagarin had been right.

The only way to avoid death is to live.

I jumped from the plane. Above my head, lined against the clear blue of the sky, the snow-white parachute billowed out. With a jerk it arrested my free fall.

I realised I'd not got round to asking Huck who'd done it. Who did 'kill' Ľudka? Who was that mysterious almighty, immune to justice under any regime? The plane above my head soon vanished, the roar of its engines fell away and with it the urgency of the question.

That person had a name, surname, mother, father, he'd gone to school, to work. In a manner he was even capable of loving. Like me, like you, like everyone. Or perhaps not. Maybe he had no name, no mother, no face or heart even. Just a human being. Like me, like you, like all of us.

Hassan Hussein Awni, when asked by Róbert Kirchhoff in the film of the Cervanová Case why he had lied, said:

"He who tells the truth will not be happy... If you slink about like a fox, you may enjoy a peaceful life."

I don't know.

As far as my eye could see there was just unperturbed, motionless desert.

What a beautiful day…

Let us rejoice!

So such are we, Marina of mine!
like flowers set in chilling earth,
like shooting stars, those flames divine,
like gemstones of enormous worth.

Stars fell away and so shall we,
flowers fade, and so shall you and me,
and jewels lie hidden 'neath the soil.

And yet - the stars _did_ flicker and flash,
and, mind, the flowers _did_ cut a dash,
and a diamond, though hidden,
can _NEVER_ spoil.

Andrej Sládkovič

212

֎

For a little while after I had finished reading, the walls of the house in which I have spent my life repeated after me: "So such we are, so such we are..." The rays of the sun were already hammering impatiently on the wooden shutters like early-morning regulars on the door of their local before opening time.

I stood up. The undertakers would be along soon.

My husband was never a good sleeper, he would keep tossing and turning or going to the toilet. That night his blanket hadn't moved one little bit. It wouldn't be long before that for which he had long been preparing, after which he had hankered so obsessively, would come to pass. He would be once more "part of the cosmic dust".

A strip of light broke in through a chink in the shutter, and through the particles of white dust it traced a laser line in the air. Inside the open wardrobe it bounced back off something metallic.

I found it. Two little figurines right at the back of the shelf. Identical. A soldier with a machine gun and an heroically thrust-out chest. Across the base it said, in Russian letters:

Stand to the last!

So such...
So...
Such...
...are...
...we.
We are.
Were.
We?
Were we?
Will we be?
So...

"Soooooo!" The scream, suppressed for centuries, issued from my throat.

The metal in which the two objects were cast was colder than all the retributions of the world. In my hands they grew red hot, I turned into lava, my heart belched out molten primeval mud, Mount Saint Helens, Mount Fuji, Krakatoa, they all sprang to life at the same instant and I started hitting him, hitting, hitting, bashing away at that cold, pale face and the two Stalingrad witnesses left deep, dark, deserved dents in the dead man's head.

"So! So! So! Soo! Soo! Sooo!

"Soooooooo!"

I grabbed him by the grey hair over his ears and kept banging his flagging head on the pillow on which it lay until, exhausted, I collapsed onto his face. I was sobbing, trying to catch my breath like someone just saved from drowning, but still clutching his hair in my clenched fists.

His hair ... The silver hair that had made him so irresistible.

Why did this talented, wise and admirable man not become what he could have become? Why had he evolved into that wretched misanthrope instead? Why didn't he ever trust me, tell me, accept me? Love me...?

Tell me: why? Is this the decency you so sought? Why didn't you simply let yourself be happy, let yourself be loved?

I cried and cried. And with me all the women in his life. Elena, Nina, Monika, Klára, Lucia, they were all there with me, crying. Our tears silently cooled the lava flows, and the stony bitumen of the earth now gave off a pleasant warmth.

I've no idea how long we lay over him like that before I grabbed that Gaudeamus thing and we all went downstairs.

All but one.

The coals in the grate first inspected the bundle of papers with mistrust, then burst into flames with a whoosh and the whole house was flooded with the bright light. A powerful gust of air fluttered the pages, blew out the candles, parted the curtains and nudged the windows and door open.

It only took ten seconds to subdue that flash of eternity.

I brushed the ashes onto the shovel. There even the last, still legible, black letters on the velvet of the burnt paper disintegrated into barren dust.

I'll leave the window open. The place needs a good airing.

When I returned upstairs, there she was. Sitting beside the bed, looking at him, silently. After a while, a voice came, a voice as calm as a moonlit lake, as soft as a distant nebula.

"He loved. As much as words can say, as much as worlds can imagine. And he let himself to be loved. Oh, yes, he loved and loved to be loved. His love was like a shooting star, brief, as the beauty of flowers cut from their roots, hot and bright, like a diamond etching the darkness of the universe."

She turned and looked at me with her dark green eyes. She was young and beautiful. In her hands was the book I just burned.

"Let us rejoice!" she said.

She looked through my body as if addressing the never-ending flow of souls wandering across all the heavens and hells since the beginning of time.

"Let us rejoice!" she repeated.

The rays of the sun roamed mischievously about the house, inspecting everything they alighted on with curiosity, as if contemplating what other figments might be conceived here.

There was a little glint coming from her left hand. Yes, she had a gold ring on her fourth finger with a constellation of tiny diamonds.

A little box lay open on the edge of the bed.

"Love," she said quietly. *"Love is the eternity. Love is joy."*

I looked at my deceased husband. His face, still pale and wounded, seemed to be smiling.

AFTERWORD

Gaudeamus:

Fact-Fiction-Fantasy – a Three-dimensional Tragicomedy

Richard's only novel – and I don't hesitate to call it one – cannot fail to fascinate the reader at every turn, from the structure marked out in the opening pages to the cliff-hanging conclusion and the nagging suspicion that there is more here than meets the eye.

The work's physical history is only one of many odd features that underlie its origins, first publication in Slovak and its ultimate translation into English.

The author is not known as a writer by profession; he is a Slovak doctor working in London. During his lifetime he has perforce experienced all that a man of his generation has had to, having lived in a fairly regimented Soviet-bloc country with compulsory military service and having followed a career liable to be fraught with bureaucracy and infighting both before and after the changes that came about in 1989, and, since those changes, having witnessed all the things that might (and did) go wrong owing to the mismanagement, opportunism, gangsterdom and other negative features that accompanied the early decades following the country's switch to a modern 'capitalist' economy with a democratic gloss. The book is the product of a nagging urge to set down one way or another many of the aspects of the last half-century in the history of (Czecho-)Slovakia – and one story in particular, the 'Ludmila' case. I say 'one way or another' because while the book includes verifiable facts from the author's lifetime experience – though the unequivocally autobiographical is, as with most authors, hard to filter out, it is clearly also fictional, derived both from the author's particular skill as a story-teller and from his knack of switching without warning to some quite amazing flights of fancy/fantasy. Not to mention the element of sci-fi in the later part of the main narrative.

The purely fictional aspect is set fair and square by the book's structure: it consists of a fairly short first-person framework narrative spoken/recorded, as it were in real time, by the recent (by hours) widow of a domineering husband as she keeps vigil overnight until the hearse can come next morning. She is occupying herself by reading a manuscript that she has found, purporting to be a narrative set down by a colleague of her husband, a man so individualised as to be called *Kolega* (capital K) in the original as if by name. The reading matter then becomes the substance of the novel, completely outweighing the widow's preamble and brief interpolations at different times during her reading.

(Whether one night is enough for her to have read and digested the typescript is a moot point.) The widow and the reader are equally entitled to wonder whether the entire text isn't actually purely alibistic: is her late husband actually his own Colleague, or not? This merely adds to the work's dimension as mystery, but is not in any sense a determining dubiety.

Within this structure the text includes what we must crudely call chapter headings in the form of an impressive range of Latin tags. Although the educated Central European will be familiar with rather more of these than the average British reader (even one from within the public school or Oxbridge purlieu), the author included in the original edition, as an appendix, a full list of them with their translation (even those that barely need it), though without giving their Classical source, unlike the many other telling quotations that appear in the text, drawn from a wide range of sources. This part of the book's apparatus is, I believe, neither obtrusive nor redundant and is matched in full in the present translation. Having digested each heading (following a check with the appendix as and when found necessary), the reader cannot fail to be struck by how magnificently apt each one is to the passage that follows it. It should be noted that as a factor contributing to the sense of alibism as regards the notional protagonist of the main narrative – the deceased or his colleague – all the headings are presented (and so seen and read by the widow, and reproduced in our printed record of the typescript record that she is reading) as handwritten insertions made ex post by her husband, wherever he had found the space for them: some are to the left, some centred, some to the right and extending into the margin, or indeed scribbled in the margin at right-angles to the text itself (incidentally constituting a typesetting nightmare!). The book's title itself is taken from one such tag, as the title of the Latin students' anthem, *Gaudeamus igitur*, and alternates – in light of the story that unfolds and in the course of that unfolding – between befitting the deeply inset core context and being charged with infinite irony. It is also, incidentally, one of those book titles that, being in a third language, raise no problems when it comes to translation (compare this to the situation mentioned in the final paragraph below).

I have already mentioned briefly the original Slovak edition. For reasons not unconnected with the sheer sensitivity of the unresolved murder that is – I feel sure – what drove the author's urge to give written expression to an event of which he had (firsthand?) experience, and with the history and, here, the implied criticism, of the equivocal handling of the case by the Slovak courts, both before and after the Changes (even the European Court of Human Rights became involved), it was perhaps impossible or injudicious for any domestic publisher to take on this emotionally and politically charged work. Accordingly its only appearance in print was as a private printing produced ("for friends and friends of friends") through Facebook. (I would be the last to dismiss it, on those grounds alone, as a mere instance of vanity publishing.) Consequently it will be found in no catalogues, nor is an internet search likely to turn it up, and of course it could not have had an ISBN. This said, it does exist as a limited edition circulating among a smallish readership and there was, then, a material object, a book, from which the present translation could be made (since completion of the translation the author has actually made some small additions and deletions by which the English text now differs from the original); such evidence as there is suggests that it has been well received by those who have seen it. The actual 1976 murder case (or simple disappearance or abduction of the girl, Ľudmila Cervanová, alleged to have been murdered) that becomes the narrative's tragic linchpin remains for many unresolved. Discussion of the case in the Slovak media came back with a vengeance on 13 June 2017, when the respected journalist Martin Hanus wrote a 7,600-word piece for the daily *Postoj*, explaining why he now believes that those charged with the real Ľudmila's murder were indeed guilty, though previously he had gone with the opposite view. Predictably, the hundreds of responses to the on-line version of the article are split between unreserved praise for Hanus' admission of his previous error and virulent abuse from those who believe he has been manipulated. *Plus ça change…*

So, the central narrative offers a fictional rendering of a range of autobiographical and socio-historical facts from the lifetime of one who undergoes every conceivable mutation as he progresses from Young Pioneer-hood, through military service, employment as a military then national health service doctor to an entrepreneur with an impressive, if spookily fantastical invention to his credit. As if human folly were not source enough to provide for a bitter, bittersweet or wildly comical portrayal of aspects of Slovak life and society at different times in the last half-century, we are treated, as noted, to some even alarming departures into fantasy that actually facilitate the image of (predominantly) the

ills that accompany this or that underlying event or set of circumstances. And because, at core, sex is probably what underlay
the disappearance/murder of the missing girl, sex also rears its
often alarmingly grotesque head (pun quite intended!) in many
of the fantasy sections. It is some of these parts that have been
toned down between the original and the translation.

The reader will be quite capable him-/herself of deciding what
s/he does or does not find offensive, improbable, comical etc. etc.
If I were to express a predilection of my own, it would be for the
digs (not necessarily entirely original or unique, though I have
yet to meet the likes of some of them elsewhere) at the ways of
the Soviets and of hardliners in the Czechoslovak Union of Youth
(an arm of the Communist Party of Czechoslovakia). I particularly relished the handling of the boneheaded, narrow-minded,
sycophantic idiocy of the *politruk* of one Soviet delegation, who
reminded me so much of another of his ilk who accompanied a
group visiting Birmingham in the mid-1960s when I was a student of Russian there and had been invited by the (now defunct)
Educational Interchange Council to act as interpreter for the
group. (Another *politruk* I had dealings with within the USSR
merely greased his utter ignorance of everything with smarm.)

Another beautifully crafted portrayal of a period feature is the
sheer guile with which conscripts of the Czechoslovak People's
Army rise to the occasion when required to put on a show (po-
liticised culture or 'culture' being of no small importance to the
then regime in all walks of life), starting from their selection
of Pushkin's notionally harmless epic fairy tale of Ruslan and
Ludmila, which could not fail to meet with official approval since

it is Russian in origin and Pushkin had always been in good odour. And of course it suits the author perfectly given his engagement with the Ľudmila Cervanová case: both Ludmila and Ľudmila are, or may have been, abducted. (Some might say that attacking the regime's military is like kicking a dead horse, as when Jaroslav Hašek took up his pen against Austria-Hungary in *The Adventures of the Good Soldier Schweik* only after the target was dead and gone and so not amenable to improvement by satire. More recently, compare this with, say, among others, Miroslav Švandrlík's *Black Barons* of 1969. The case of *Gaudeamus* is redeemed, however, by the still-live thread of the Cervanová case.)

To summarise in the crudest terms: I found this a highly engaging book, sometimes a difficult read and not always easy to translate, and one that is quite striking for its sheer variety of themes and modes of narration. As an introduction to the last fifty years of Slovak history and society it is only as 'historical' as the limited range and tacit interpretation of the facts included permit, the factual being far outweighed by the fictional and fantastical. It is a work of true imagination to which a reader might happily return.

DAVID SHORT
Windsor, July 2017

APPENDIX

Notes for the enquiring reader on names, institutions and quotations that may not be instantly known or recognised.

p. 5 *et passim* **Jozef Tiso** (1887-1947): Roman Catholic priest, leader of the Slovak People's Party, sole president of the wartime Slovak State (a German puppet), finally executed as a traitor.

-- **Gustáv Husák** (1913-91): Slovak Communist politician who rose to become secretary general of the Czechoslovak Communist Party and President of the Czechoslovak Socialist Republic (1975-89).

-- **Miroslav Válek** (1927-91): Slovak poet, publicist and politician, who eventually rose to the position of Minister of Culture.

-- **Alexander Dubček** (1921-92): Slovak Communist politician who became the leading light of the reforming movement that came to be known as the Prague Spring. After the Soviet occupation of 1968 he was eventually reduced to a job in forestry, only returning to politics, if briefly, after the fall of communism in 1989.

-- **Good-for-nothing** (Slovak *Popolvár*): A much-loved fairy-tale character known thanks to the work of the Protestant clergyman Pavol Dobšinský (1828-85), a hugely energetic revivalist collector and editor of a vast body of Slovak folk literature. After great adventures involving magic, liberating beautiful princesses from the clutches of many-headed dragons and much else besides Good-for-nothing successfully belies his nickname. The story's full title is 'The Greatest Good-for-nothing in the World', which already hints at the antithesis between name and deeds.

pp. 6 and 121 **Velimir Khlebnikov** (1885-1922): Russian Futurist poet, on whom see, for a potted characterisation, https://en.wikipedia.org/wiki/Velimir_Khlebnikov. One of his best-known poems comes on p.70.

p. 39 ***Timur and his Team***: Soviet film (1940) about a selfless group of boys who help families whose menfolk are at the front or have died. Often sneered at outside the USSR as excessively PC in the Soviet manner.

p. 44 **Schweik Tavern**: Named after the Good Soldier Schweik, 'hero' of Jaroslav Hašek's rambling novel about the First World War. Schweik became a byword in Czech – and further afield (see, *inter alia*, the OED) – for deviously getting the better of authority, especially the military authorities. The novel has been – with very mixed success – translated several times into English. One of Schweik's catchwords is *To chce klid*, roughly equivalent to 'Take it easy', 'Keep your hair on', etc.

p. 46 **Becherovka**: This golden bitter liqueur in its traditional green bottle might fairly be called a Czechoslovakian classic. It is made in Carlsbad – Karlovy Vary in Western Bohemia and is now owned by Pernod. Some would say that this is one of the tragedies of the no-holds-barred capitalism that followed the fall of Communism.

p. 47 *et passim* **Yuri Gagarin** (1934-68): The first and still best-remembered Soviet cosmonaut (space trip in 1961), celebrated by, amongst others, a monument created by the husband and wife team of Czech sculptors Antonín Kuchař and Gisela Zubrová-Kuchařová and erected in the centre of the spa town of Karlovy Vary in 1975. It was removed to the airport in 1992. (Most flights from this airport go to Moscow, Russian 'entrepreneurs' having taken over much of Karlovy

Vary.) Czechoslovakia was the first foreign country Gagarin visited, and he made several times trips to Karlovy Vary. See, for example, https://www.karlovyvary.cz/cs/pomnik-juri-je-gagarina for an image of the monument.

p. 57 **Karel Kryl** (1944-94): the Czech Bob Dylan, hugely followed during the 'Prague Spring' for his merciless attacks on the follies of the Communist regime; with time he was – quite understandably – barely less critical of the Czech(oslovak) version of capitalism that followed it after 1989.

p. 57 *et passim* **ARAB**: an acronym widely used by National Servicemen conscripted into the British Army until the early 1960s. The acronym shortens the phrase 'Arrogant Regular Army Bastard'.

-- *Bratříčku, nevzlykej, to nejsou bubáci, vždyť jsi už velikej, to jsou jen vojáci...* – Czech: 'Brother, stop sobbing, they're not spooks, you're a big boy now, they're only soldiers...' [Karel Kryl]

-- *Ya nye sovyetskii, ya tolko russkii, ya peterburskii anarchist...* – Russian: 'I'm not Soviet, I'm just a Russian, I'm a St Petersburg anarchist...'

-- *menya zanyali, v Sibir poslali, patamu shto nye communist!* – Russian: 'they captured me, sent me to Siberia, because I'm not a communist!'

p. 58 **_kérem szépen_** – Hungarian: 'please'.

-- **_persze, biztos_** – Hungarian: 'of course', 'sure, certainly'.

p. 59 **_The zip slid down the small of your back..._** From 'Sanguine' by Jacques Prévert, translated from the French by Phoebe Power, see http://www.ismla.co.uk/newsletter/ ISMLASpring2012.pdf.

p. 60 **_Ruslan and Ludmila_** – A favorite among Russian tales, Ruslan and Ludmila was written in poetic form by Russia's most beloved writer, Alexander Pushkin. It was later the basis of Glinka's most successful opera. In brief: Once upon a time, in a land far away there was a great feast celebrating the marriage of the land's greatest warrior, Ruslan, to the land's most beautiful maiden, Ludmila. But tragedy happened upon the feast when the bride was kidnapped by the dwarf magician Chernomor. Enraged, Ludmila's father declared that only the warrior who rescues his daughter would be her husband

Ruslan and his rivals Farlaf, Ratmir, and Rogdai prepared to rescue the beautiful girl. Only Ruslan understood that he would have to overcome great feats and magical powers to rescue his bride. Rogdai killed Ratmir and then attacked Ruslan. But Ruslan won the fight, and threw Rogdai into the River Dnieper. Ruslan wandered further into the unknown where he entered a thick fog and came upon a giant magic head. Underneath the head was a knife, which he knew he must retrieve. Ruslan defeated the head and took the knife. He then was able to defeat Chernomor. He used this knife to cut off the dwarf's beard, thus having diminished the dwarf's magical powers.

Having defeated Chernomor, Ruslan found his bride in a magical garden, he rescued Ludmila and took her back to the feast where they were finally married.

-- *Persze hogy pamätám.* – A hybrid Hungarian-Slovak utterance amounting to 'Of course I remember', followed by the Hungarian version of the name of Alexander Pushkin.

-- *Talpra Magyar, hí a haza!* – The first line of the most famous poem by Sándor Petőfi, known generally as "Talpra Magyar". It means "Magyars, rise, your country calls you!"

p. 62 *Horror – the girl he loved had gone!* – Translation by Roger Clarke, v. http://www.almaclassics.com/excerpts/Ruslan_Lyudmila.pdf, p.13/15.

p. 63 *And to whom do I...*, *Those card-carrying swindlers...* and p. 155 *Was it then? No, further back than that...* – M. Válek: *Slovo*, 1976.

p. 65 *lacipecsenye* – Untranslatable name of a kind of once popular street-food version of barbecued pork steaks.

-- *Egészségünkre* – Hungarian: 'Cheers!'

p. 68 **Sabinov**: A town in East Slovakia; the former military prison is now subsidiary to the large non-military prison in Prešov.

p. 71 *Oh Barbara...* – Translation © Lawrence Ferlinghetti; adopted from http://www.boppin.com/poets/prevert.htm. Jacques Prévert (1900-77), French poet and screenwriter, whose poems have been somewhat randomly translated into English, but several of whose screenplays, such as *Les Enfants du Paradis* (1945), have been and still are highly regarded.

p. 81 *Run away home, Ivan,...* Translation after J. Vomáčka, *Well-meant advice*. http://www.akordytexty.sk/index.php?id_skladby=7n5lxyr&act=detail [9 November 2014]

p. 99 *Ai, zde leží zem ta,...* -- from Jan Kollár's *Slávy dcera* (1824)

-- *The total current entering a junction must equal the total current leaving the junction; the sum of the squares on the hypotenuse is equal to the sum of the squares on the other two sides; a body immersed in a fluid...* – respectively Kirchhoff' first law, 1845; Pythagoras' Theorem, ca. 500 B.C., and [first words of] Archimedes' Law, ca. 250 B.C.

-- *Ω ΞΕΙΝ, ΑΓΓΕΛΛΕΙΝ ΛΑΚΕΔΑΙΜΟΝΙΟΙΣ ΟΤΙ ΤΗΔΕ...* – Simonides: *Epitaph*, ca. 500 B.C.

-- *Проглас ѥсмь свѧтоу єѵаньгелию...* – Constantine the Philosopher: *Proglas*, 863-867 A.D.

-- *Ceterum censeo Carthaginem esse delendam!* – Cato, ca. 157 B.C.

-- *Я к вам пишу — чего же боле?...* Aleksander Sergeyevich Pushkin: *Eugene Onegin.*

-- *Liberté, égalité, fraternité!* – M. de Robespierre: *Discours sur l'organisation des gardes nationals (1790)*

-- *Sur le pont d'Avignon...* – French folk song ca. 1450.

p. 100 *London's burning...* – English folk song, post-1666.

-- *Freude, schöner Götterfunken,...* – Friedrich Schiller: *An die Freude* (Ode to Joy), 1785.

-- *Cogito, ergo sum!* – René Descartes: *Discours de la méthode*, 1637.

-- *Marína moja!...* – Andrej Sládkovič: *Marína*, 1844. Andrej Sládkovič (1820-72), whose name figures here and there in the book, was a Protestant clergyman, poet, translator and literary critic, hugely important in the history of Slovak literature, a much-loved classic, not least of all for his patriotic bent. *Marína* is considered the all-time best Slovak love poem; it is about the poet's unrequited love for the socially unequal Marína Pischlová.

p. 101 **Gaudeamus igitur...** – The student song properly known as *De brevitate vitae*, 1287.

p. 122 **And this, O men of Athens...** – Plato: *Defence of Socrates*, adapted from Benjamin Jowett's translation at http://classics.mit.edu/Plato/apology.html.

p. 154 **'The hour of departure...'** – translation borrowed from http://classics.mit.edu/Plato/apology.html.

-- **Koyaanisqatsi** – Hopi: 'Life out of balance.' (See the eponymous 1982 film by Godfrey Reggio.)

-- **Samsara** – a 2011 documentary film directed by Ron Fricke and produced by Mark Magidson (v. https://en.wikipedia.org/wiki/Samsara_(2011_film).

-- **Nos habebit humus, nemini parcetur** – The soil will have us; none shall be spared (i.e. a line from *Gaudeamus igitur*)

p. 171 **We, the people of Slovakia,...** – from the Constitution of the Slovak Republic, 1992.

-- **We the peoples of the United Nations...** – UN Charter, 1945.

-- **We, men of Athens...** – Plato: *Defence of Socrates.*

-- **We want nothing foreign…** – Jozef Tiso, Slovak wartime leader, 1939 (v.s.).

-- **We're not like them!** – Anon, 1989.

-- **Who is not with us is against us!** – Klement Gottwald, first Communist president of Czechoslovakia, 1948.

p. 175 **O, laugh, ye laughers! …** – Velimir Khlebnikov: *Invocation of Laughter*. (For another more literal translation see http:// www.poemhunter.com/poem/invocation-of-laughter/.)

p. 177 **Do Truth and Love have to prevail over lies and hatred?** A reference to the assertion by, or motto of, the former dissident and late president of the Czechoslovak Republic, Václav Havel, that they do.

p. 188 **Neque porro quisquam est qui dolorem ipsum quia dolor sit amet, consectetur, adipisci velit…** – Cicero: There is no one who loves pain itself, who seeks after it and wants to have it, simply because it is pain.

-- **Lorem ipsum** – A version of the kind of cod Latin filler text used in typography, see, for example, https://en.wikipedia. org/wiki/Lorem_ipsum.

p. 213 **So such we are, my dear…** – A direct reference to Sládkovič's *Marína* (v.s.). Cf. the section of the poem quoted on p. 214.

Also available from Jantar Publishing

FOX SEASON
AND OTHER SHORT STORIES
by Agnieszka Dale

Agnieszka Dale's characters all want to find greatness, but they realise greatness isn't their thing. But what is? And what is great anyway? In *Peek-a-boo*, a mother breastfeeds her child via Skype, at work. In *Hello Poland*, a man reunites with his daughter in a world where democracy has been replaced by user testing. In other short stories, people bow and are bowed to. They feed foxes or go fishing. They kiss the fingers of those they love while counting to ten.

CHILDREN OF OUR AGE
by A.M. Bakalar

Karol and his wife are the rising stars of the Polish community in London but Karol is a ruthless entrepreneur whose fortune is built on the backs of his fellow countrymen. The Kulesza brothers, mentally unstable Igor and his violent brother Damian, dream about returning to Poland one day. A loving couple, Mateusz and Angelika, believe against all odds that good things will happen to people like them. Gradually, all of these lives become dramatically entwined, and each of them will have to decide how far they are willing to go in pursuit of their dreams.

www.jantarpublishing.com

Also available from Jantar Publishing

BURYING THE SEASON
by Antonín Bajaja

Translated from the Czech by David Short

An affectionate, multi-layered account of small town life in central
Europe beginning in the early 1930s and ending in the 21st Century.
Adapting scenes from Fellini's *Amarcord*, Bajaja's meandering narrative
weaves humour, tragedy and historical events into a series of compelling
nostalgic anecdotes.

BLISS WAS IT IN BOHEMIA
by Michal Viewegh

Translated from the Czech by David Short

A wildly comic story about the fate of a Czech family from the 1960s
onwards. At turns humorous, ironic and sentimental, an engaging
portrait of their attempts to flee from history (meaning the 1968
Soviet invasion of Czechoslovakia) – or at least to ignore it as long as
possible… Light-hearted and sophisticated at once, this is a book that
reminds us that comedy can tackle large historical subjects successfully.

www.jantarpublishing.com

Also available from Jantar Publishing

A KINGDOM OF SOULS
by Daniela Hodrová

Translated from the Czech by Véronique Firkusny and Elena Sokol

Through playful poetic prose, imaginatively blending historical and cultural motifs with autobiographical moments, Daniela Hodrová shares her unique perception of Prague. *A Kingdom of Souls* is the first volume of this author's literary journey — an unusual quest for self, for one's place in life and in the world, a world that for Hodrová is embodied in Prague.

PRAGUE. I SEE A CITY...
by Daniela Hodrová

Translated from the Czech by David Short

Originally commissioned for a French series of alternative guidebooks, Hodrová's novel is a conscious addition to the tradition of Prague literary texts by, for example, Karel Hynek Mácha, Jakub Arbes, Gustav Meyrink and Franz Kafka, who present the city as a hostile living creature or labyrinthine place of magic and mystery in which the individual human being may easily get lost.

www.jantarpublishing.com

Also available from Jantar Publishing

THREE FACES OF AN ANGEL
by Jiří Pehe

Translated from the Czech by Gerald Turner

Three Faces of an Angel is a novel about the twentieth century that begins when time was linear and ended when the notion of progress was less well defined. The Brehmes' story guides the reader through revolution, war, the holocaust, and ultimately exile and return. A novel about what man does to man and whether God intervenes.

GRAVELARKS
by Jan Křesadlo

Translated from the Czech by Václav Z J Pinkava

Zderad, a noble misfit, investigates a powerful party figure in 1950s Czechoslovakia. His struggle against blackmail, starvation and betrayal leaves him determined to succeed where others have failed and died. Set in Stalinist era Central Europe, *GraveLarks* is a triumphant intellectual thriller navigating the fragile ambiguity between sado-masochism, black humour, political satire, murder and hope.

www.jantarpublishing.com

Also available from Jantar Publishing

KYTICE

CZECH & ENGLISH BILINGUAL EDITION

by Karel Jaromír Erben

Translated from the Czech by Susan Reynolds

Kytice was inspired by Erben's love of Slavonic myth and the folklore surrounding such creatures as the Noonday Witch and the Water Goblin. First published in 1853, these poems, along with Mácha's *Máj* and Němcová's *Babička*, are the best loved and most widely read 19th century Czech classics. Published in the expanded 1861 version, the collection has moved generations of artists and composers, including Dvořák, Smetana and Janáček.

www.jantarpublishing.com